THE MORNING OF THE GODS

Edward Fenton

The Morning of the Gods

Julia MacRae Books

A DIVISION OF FRANKLIN WATTS

© 1987 Edward Fenton
All rights reserved
First published in Great Britain
1987 by Julia MacRae Books
A division of Franklin Watts
12a Golden Square, London, W1R 4BA
and Franklin Watts Australia
14 Mars Road, Lane Cove, N.S.W. 2066

Designed by Douglas Martin
Typesetting by Computape (Pickering) Ltd
Printed and bound in Great Britain by
Billings of Worcester

British Library Cataloguing in Publication Data
Fenton, Edward, *1917–*
The morning of the gods.
I. Title
823'.914[F]   PZ7

ISBN 0–86203–293–8

Contents

"Belovéd Pan . . ."

1 *The Asphodel Fields*

Carla stared out through the window of the bus at the Greek landscape rushing past. It was so stark: as bare as the bones of the earth, like nothing she had ever seen before. If only there were something familiar in it, something that she could hold on to! The photographs that her mother had shown her had not prepared her for this. Greece was her mother's country. The photographs had been a part of her mother's life, not Carla's.

Even though her mother had been born in another country, Carla had never travelled before. She had spent her whole life in New York, in the same Manhattan apartment. Every summer they had gone to the same rented cottage in Vermont. Once her father had taken her along to Washington when he was working on a civil rights case, and twice she had spent spring vacation on Long Island with her friend Honor's family. Now she was on a bus on her way to a Greek village. All she knew about it was its name. Overhead, there was the Greek sky with its incredibly clear light. Ismene, her mother, had always described it in that special, intense voice she used when she talked about Greece. "You will see it all for yourself," she used to say, "when I take you there."

"That's what you always say," Carla would tell her. "But when?"

"When the time is right."

"And when will that be?"

"As soon as the Colonels have gone and it's a free country again."

"Those Colonels! You're always going on about them. Who are they, really?"

Ismene's face tightened as it always did when she mentioned them. "They are a group of professional military men," she said, "a Junta as they call it, who took over the country. They run everything by military law. Greece is a dictatorship now. There's no freedom of thought."

"You mean they can stop you from thinking?" Carla asked.

"No," she answered, pushing Carla's dark hair back off Carla's forehead. "But they stop you from *saying* what you think." Carla had stood there, staring at her mother. She could not possibly imagine anyone stopping Ismene from saying what she thought.

Now, in 1974, she had finally come to Greece, even though the Colonels' Junta was still in power after seven years; even though her mother wasn't there to show it to her.

In the midst of all the confusion at the Athens airport, a young man had met her. Actually, when she got a good look at him, he was not so young.

"Miss Carla Lewis?"

It wasn't a question, he seemed to have known at once who she was. Maybe she should have brushed her hair before getting off the plane. "Welcome to Greece," he said.

Pinned to the lapel of his blue jacket was a pair of silver wings with the words HERMES TOURS above them. He even had short curly hair that made him look like the famous statue of Hermes, the messenger of the Gods, in her parents' book of ancient Greek art.

He scooped up her suitcase and waved her past the customs men, into the hard glare of the Greek day. "Tiggie and Theo sent me word from the village to look after you," he said. "It's too bad that there won't be time to show you the Acropolis." She did catch a brief glimpse of it from his little car. It floated like a marble birthday cake above the ugly concrete buildings and the frantic traffic of the city.

Then he had put her on the bus. A woman was boarding it at the same time. She had white hair, but her face was unlined, so it was hard to tell exactly how old she was. She was hung with parcels, and carried a covered wicker basket. Leather sandals were bound to her swollen ankles. Her hair was tied in a tight bandeau. From her neck hung a necklace of Egyptian scarabs, and she wore two curious bracelets in the shape of snakes with eyes of shiny black stone. When the Hermes man asked her in Greek if she wouldn't mind keeping an eye on Carla, she simply reached out, grabbed her by the wrist, and towed her on board. Then, before Carla could thank him, the messenger of the Gods flashed her a quick smile and vanished. It was as though he had vaporised.

The woman, enthroned on the seat beside her, set the wicker basket on her wide lap. Every so often she bent over and whispered to it. What could be inside? Suddenly, the lid was pushed open an inch or two and a small ginger-and-white paw emerged. It waved about restlessly, exploring the air.

"He hates to travel," the woman said. "He doesn't take to being confined."

"Maybe he just wants to look at the world," Carla said. "I could hold him for you."

The woman had large, rather popping eyes. *The Python Lady*, Carla thought, because of the bracelets she wore. She reached into the basket and drew out a ginger cat with enormous blue eyes. She put it in Carla's lap, where it settled like a small sphinx, purring loudly while it too watched out of the window.

By now the bus driver had a cassette going full blast. Loud Greek songs were pouring out of it, so that it was difficult to hear the Python Lady's questions. "How old are you? . . . Where do you come from? . . . How is it that you can speak Greek?"

"My mother . . ." Carla began, and broke off.

Ever since that day when she had been called to the principal's office at school to find her father waiting to tell her about the car accident and that her mother was dead, talking to other people was like making signals through glass, signals that no one would answer. It was like the poem Mrs Schoenberger had read to them in English class, about a man who was far out in the water. They thought he was waving. Only it turned out that he wasn't waving, he was drowning.

Her father had made an appointment for her to see a fatherly-looking man, a psychiatrist. His voice poured over her like syrup.

"Wouldn't you like to talk about what is troubling you, Carla?"

"Not particularly."

"Would you care to tell me about your mother?"

"No."

"What would you like to talk to me about, then?"

"Nothing."

"Nothing? You mean nothing is troubling you?"

"No. I mean there's nothing I particularly want to talk about."

"Not even to me? I might be able to help you. That's what I'm here for."

"I know that. And I know that it's very expensive coming here. But I don't want to discuss it with you."

Sitting there, in his office filled with antiques, she had thought: my mother is dead. I will never see her again.

That was the end of it. What was there to talk about?

Then why did she find herself answering the Python Lady's questions? Was it because the Python Lady was a stranger, someone she would probably never see again? Or was it because she had spoken to her in Greek, the way her mother had?

"I'm thirteen," she said. "Almost fourteen. I got here today from New York. My mother was Greek. When I was little she sent me to a special class in New York to learn the language."

The Python Lady said, "You learned it very well."

"What surprises me, though, is that I understand more than I expected."

"You often understand more than you expect," said the Python Lady.

There was a pause. Carla and the ginger cat watched the scenery slide by.

"What brings you here, my child? And why are you travelling alone?"

"I have come here on a visit," she replied.

"I see," the Python Lady said, as though she knew that there was more to it than that.

Carla was ready to tell her more. But even though the Greek words kept coming back to her, the music on the cassette player was so loud that it wasn't easy for her to be heard above it. She wanted to tell the Python Lady about Ismene: how even on a crowded street she seemed different from everyone else; how, although she was small, only two inches taller than Carla, there was always something about her, like a bright scarf, to make her stand out. Carla liked to think she looked a little like her mother: the black, black hair; the olive skin; the pointed face with the dark eyes that seemed to fill it. It was on account of her Greek mother that Carla was never in exactly the same mould as the other girls at her school no matter what she did to her hair or how she was dressed. There were times when she envied her best friend, Honor, who had fair, wavy hair and blue eyes. Honor came from what she called "an old New York family". She never questioned anything. It seemed natural to Honor to live in an old brownstone town house. "Doesn't everybody? Oh, I don't mean you, Carla. You're different." Honor said, "You know, my mother is a typical B. Altman customer. When I was little I used to ask her where I came from, and she used to say, 'Why, we just went down to Altman's on the Fifth Avenue bus and picked you out!'" Honor's father was also a lawyer, like Carla's father, but Mr Beekman was a partner in his old family firm. His speciality was corporation law and taking care of estates. He never got involved in civil rights causes like Carla's father, or had clients who didn't have enough money to pay his fees. Carla's father was always saying that being a lawyer was a sacred trust, something like being a doctor. You had to do what you could for people whether they could pay you or not.

It was her mother who made everything different for Carla in New York. Wherever they went, people asked Ismene, "Are you Spanish? Or French?"

"No. I am Greek."

And she made slips in English that made Carla and her father laugh, like the time she was arguing with Carla's father and cried, "Oh, you and your American daughter! You are forever gangstering up on me!"

Being with Ismene was never like doing things with her father. He took her out to men's places, like the dining room of his university club, or the Oyster Bar at Grand Central. He would tell her about his newest case, or his college days, or the time he had been a part of the civil rights protests in Alabama. Sometimes she wondered if he really wished she had been a boy.

Honor was sure that Carla was wrong about that. But then, Honor had two brothers, one of them already at law school. Her father always made a special fuss over her because she was the only girl in the family. He never talked to Honor the way Carla's father talked to her.

Going out with her mother was what her father referred to with a wry grin as "going off to join the Greek Underground". Whenever they were in a restaurant, her mother would know at once from the waiter's accent if he was Greek, and then say something to him in his language. When Carla was small, it used to embarrass her, but as she grew older, it was fun. After that, they would be served at once, with a special flourish, while everyone else would be kept waiting. It was the same with taxis. If the driver happened to be Greek, the ride always turned out to be an adventure. Once, the driver refused to let Ismene pay the fare because he had enjoyed talking to her so much. "It was like taking my family for a ride," he said.

There was a whole network of Greeks in their neighbourhood: the shoemaker on Lexington Avenue; the florist on Madison Avenue who always threw in an extra bunch of something for her mother; the man at the vegetable stand who let her pick and choose and who always added an apple or a tangerine for Carla; the doorman at the hotel on the next block who could be counted on to get Ismene a taxi even on the rainiest days; the saleswoman at Bloomingdale's who would spend hours with them discussing Carla's clothes. Because of her mother, the city had a special, Greek dimension that none of her friends at school knew existed, except for Honor. Honor would say, "Carla, you're so lucky being half Greek. I'm only one thing, and sometimes it can be so boring!"

Now Ismene was dead. She had left Carla stranded. Carla wasn't Greek any more; she wasn't anything. She would make a whole block's detour so as not to pass the Greek doorman and have him call out to her in Greek, "How's your mother?" She avoided the shoemaker, the coffee shop on the corner, the vegetable stand, the florist. When she needed clothes her father took her and said,

"Just pick out anything you like and charge it," which wasn't the same as going to the Greek saleswoman at Bloomingdale's with Ismene.

The Python Lady was saying, "I think you will find everything very different here from your life in New York."

"I suppose so," Carla said. But then, her life in New York was completely different now. Even her friends and teachers weren't the same towards her, after Ismene died. Honor kept saying, "How awful for you, Carla!" Even though they still saw each other every day, in and out of each other's houses, or talking on the phone, Honor didn't seem to understand how really awful it was.

Her English teacher, Mrs Schoenberger, said Carla ought to write about her mother. What was the point of it? It wouldn't bring Ismene back. It wouldn't make the apartment come to life again. Furniture got moved and it never went back exactly to the way Ismene had arranged it. Ismene had always had flowers around. Now all the vases stood around empty, collecting dust. The cleaning woman fixed the meals and they were not very exciting, just food to be eaten. All the old photographs had been put away, even Ismene's albums with the snapshots of Greece. Her father said he couldn't bear to look at them. So many small things had changed: no cigarettes on tables any more, and the telephone not ringing so often, and the laundry piling up, and clothes never properly ironed by the cleaning woman. Ismene had been terribly fussy about Carla's clothes being pressed just right. Suddenly a letter would arrive from someone who didn't know what had happened, or a magazine subscription kept coming in her mother's name, or there would be a call from somebody who had just arrived from Greece and wanted to talk to Ismene, and the awfulness returned. Her father spent less time at home. He came back late from the office, his briefcase crammed with paperwork. He didn't talk to Carla about his cases as he had with Ismene. He kept saying that they ought to go on a trip together, Bermuda, maybe, or St Thomas, but he never seemed to have the time. He hadn't taken her to the Oyster Bar or to his club for ages. He kept staying later at the office. Was it on purpose, so as not to be alone with her?

And no one laughed in the apartment any more.

She began to skip school. She would go to the movies and sit through the picture twice, or she would huddle in her room in front of the television set, staring like a zombie at whatever came on. When Honor phoned, half the time Carla said that she was too busy to talk.

One evening her father arrived home earlier than usual. "They called me today from your school," he said. "They asked me why you have been absent so often. Well? Why, Carla? What's going on? This isn't like you. I sit at work and feel you're safe and sound at school while you're really out by yourself somewhere . . . "

She shrugged. "I don't feel like going to school."

He stared at her, scratching his chin and looking angry and baffled. "And your grades are slipping. You were always such a good student. Mrs Schoenberger said you used to be the most enthusiastic girl in her class."

Carla looked down at her feet and didn't answer. It sounded as though he were talking about some other person, some girl she had heard about, maybe, or had only glimpsed in the corridors at school.

The Python Lady jolted her out of her thoughts. "And where are you going now?"

Carla told her the name of the village. "My mother's aunt lives there with her husband."

Ismene had been an only child. Her parents died when she was young and she had been brought up by her mother's sister. "I'm going to stay with my great-aunt Tiggie," Carla said.

She recalled the Sunday morning at the breakfast table

17

when her father abruptly put aside the *New York Times Book Review* and looked at her. His light brown hair was tousled and he hadn't bothered to shave yet. He would never have sat at the breakfast table like that if Ismene had been there. And that shirt he had on! She would have tossed it into the laundry basket before he had a chance to put it on again. He said, "What do you think of the idea of going to Greece?"

Greece? Without Ismene?

"When?"

"As soon as it can be arranged."

"How can I?" she said. "I have school."

"I had a long talk with Mrs Schoenberger last week. She thinks it might be a good idea for you to go, since you're not getting all that much out of school these days. You can make up for it in the fall with an extra project on Greece. A change of scene might do you good and you might as well have what she refers to as 'the Greek Experience'. Colonels or no Colonels, some of the glory that was Greece must still be around to get rubbed off on you." He smiled. "What do you think?"

"But . . . " Carla began. She had been spreading marmalade on her toast and now the spoon shook in her hand. The marmalade dribbled onto the table. She jumped up and ran into the kitchen for a sponge. How could she go to Greece, and the Colonels' Greece at that, without her mother?

"Dictators! They are Fascist dictators!" Ismene had cried. "There is no question of my setting foot in Greece so long as those Colonels are still around. I was born Greek, but while the dictatorship is still there, I am a person without a country."

When the marmalade was wiped away, Carla said, "But where will I stay?"

"I thought of sending you to Aunt Tiggie and her husband."

18

"Why should they want me? They don't even know me."

"I'm sure they'd love to have you. After all, you are Ismene's daughter."

"Do *you* want me to go? Won't you miss me?"

"Of course. I'll miss you terribly. But I'll manage. I'd be much happier about you if you were enjoying yourself with Tiggie and Theo instead of sitting in a stuffy movie house all day. And you won't be away forever. I've thought about it for days. Don't you think it's a good idea?"

"How long will I go for?"

"That depends more or less on you. You could stay on, if you liked it, until it's time to get ready for school."

From the set expression on his face she knew that he had already decided for her. "I guess it's a good idea, since you want me to go."

"Anyway," he said, "let me write to them first."

"Tiggie!" Honor had shrieked. "Like Mrs Tiggy-Winkle in Beatrix Potter?"

Carla was slightly annoyed. "No, like Antigone in the play by Sophocles that Mrs Schoenberger was talking about last week."

All the girls in Ismene's family had classical names. "But you were called after your father," Ismene had told her, "because he was so happy about you when you were born."

"And I suppose," Honor went on, "Tiggie lives in a huge apartment overlooking the Acropolis."

"As a matter of fact, she doesn't."

"Then it would be a white-washed villa on a Greek island. I wouldn't mind going myself!"

"Not that, either. She and her husband live in his village. All I know about it is that it's a sort of Greek version of Nantucket."

"Oh, Carla, lucky you! And missing school and exams and everything. How great for you!"

"Is it?" she said.

Two weeks later there was a reply to her father's letter to Greece. Theo, Tiggie's husband, wrote to say that they would be glad to have Carla come and stay with them for as long as she liked.

"Well?" her father asked. "How do you feel about it now?"

Ismene had said so many times, "When we go to Greece, Carla, I will show you everything so that you can see it for yourself."

"I think," her father said, "that your mother would have wanted you to go."

"Well, I'm going, since it's all arranged," she said at last.

"When?"

"Right away. Mrs Schoenberger said there was no objection to your leaving before spring vacation starts."

The bus had turned off the National Highway, away from the grinding trucks. The ginger sphinx was asleep in her lap. They were starting to climb. On either side of the road the fields were filled with tall spikes bearing pale, delicate flowers. They covered the stony earth like a soft cloud. She had never seen flowers like those before, not even in the Greek florist's on Madison Avenue.

The Python Lady leaned forward. "Asphodel," she said.

"Asphodel?"

"Those flowers."

How, Carla wondered, had she known she had been thinking about them?

"According to the ancient Greeks," the Python Lady said, "the asphodel was the flower of the Immortals. It bloomed in the Elysian Fields, at the ends of the earth."

Carla stared through the window. Where was she now,

if it wasn't the ends of the earth? Beyond the fields of asphodel loomed the mountain. Even though it was April, there was a layer of snow on its highest slopes.

The Python Lady said, as though she were addressing a school assembly, "The mountain of Parnassos!" Her bracelets rattled as she pointed. "Where the glorious god Apollo lives."

Lives? Perhaps Carla's Greek wasn't all that good, after all. *Lived* was probably what the Python Lady had said.

She tried to get a better look, but the Greek driver swung around the hairpin turns on the road so fast it made her dizzy. She closed her eyes. She tried to think about what lay ahead of her, at the end of this long journey. What would the village be like? And Tiggie? And Theo? She had only seen old snapshots of them.

The bus halted at a mountain village to let off some of the passengers. She could see handwoven bags and rugs hung out for sale everywhere along the narrow streets. Across the width of the village's main street stretched a banner with large black letters: GREECE FOR CHRISTIAN GREEKS.

And there was that poster again! It had been at the airport and on the concrete walls below the Acropolis. She had seen it plastered onto the smooth rocks along the highway. It was even reproduced in miniature on the driver's box of matches. It showed a soldier holding a rifle, darkly silhouetted against a blazing phoenix with outspread wings. Something about it made her shiver. Across the bottom of the poster she read the words THE TWENTY-FIRST OF APRIL.

"That was when the Colonels took over the country," the Python Lady said. She glanced quickly around her. She lowered her voice. "Colonels, generals, whatever they are," she whispered, "they all come, and eventually they all go away again." She gave Carla a strange look of complicity. "We are the ones who remain."

The bus shot off again. There was still a long stretch of mountain road ahead of them. "Soon," the Python Lady said, "we will be in Delphi." It was beginning to get dark.

"I can't wait for the day when I will show you Delphi," Ismene had said.

"There it is," the Python Lady was saying, "the home of the Delphic Oracle, the abode of Apollo, the centre of the earth!"

Carla knitted her brows. How could it possibly be that?

"You know," the Python Lady went on, "the ancient Greeks believed that Zeus, the father of the Gods, sent off two eagles from either end of the cosmos to determine the centre of the world. They met here, at Delphi. From then on it was known as the *omphalos*, the navel of the universe."

Carla caught a glimpse of the ruins of some ancient temples in the midst of thick greenery. On one side of the road yawned a deep valley. Large birds floated over it. Could they have been the eagles of Zeus, still haunting the place?

The Python Lady pointed at the steep cliffs to their right, immense bare rocks that glittered in the last rays of the departing daylight. "Those are the Phaedriades, the Shining Ones."

Carla's breath caught in her throat. Ismene had told her that pilgrims in ancient times came from all over the known world to consult the sacred oracle of Delphi, where the Sibyl waited to answer their questions. Her reply always took the form of a riddle, of something which the asker could not understand immediately. Now Carla had the feeling that in another moment the earth would shudder and split open to disclose some important mystery and that she would learn the secret of the Delphic Sibyl, whatever it was.

Then the moment passed, lost to her forever among the

souvenir shops, neon hotel signs and the rows of tourist buses that lined the main street of the modern town.

The Python Lady adjusted her bandeau. She took the cat from Carla's lap and thrust it back into the basket. She collected her overstuffed shopping bags. "This is where I leave you," she said.

Suddenly she leaned towards Carla. Her snake bracelets rattled. She fixed her popping eyes on Carla's face, and Carla suddenly felt that the woman knew the things that were, the things that had gone before, the things that would be. It was as though she might even be able to tell Carla the name of the man she would fall in love with one day. She said in a low, throaty voice, "The answer to your question is that you will find the person you are looking for."

Carla blinked at her. Had she understood? She was about to say, "But I didn't ask you any question!"

By then it was too late. The Python Lady was already waddling off the bus, clutching her bags and cradling the wicker basket that held her cat.

What had the Python Lady meant? Carla wasn't looking for anyone.

The bus moved off again. As it rushed down the snaking mountain road, there was a sudden glittering vision of the sea. Soon after that they plunged into a vast grove of gnarled olive trees. When they emerged from it, they were driving along the rocky, winding coast, through fields of asphodel. Then they were entering a village.

The driver slammed on the brakes.

There was hardly anything to see: a small square with a couple of stunted palm trees in the middle of it and some yellowish houses clutching the dry rocks; the sea behind them; and then, the vast sky.

Carla stood and took down her suitcase.

She was there. But where was Ismene, to take her by the hand and lead her into this new, unknown world?

2 *A Window on Parnassos*

Carla filed off the bus after the other passengers. A handful of people waiting outside the coffee shop in the square raked her with their eyes.

She stood there, gripping her suitcase.

An elderly couple sat at one of the little iron tables in front of the coffee house. Now they stood up. The man was tall and his white moustache gave him a vaguely military air. He might have been a retired naval officer, in his light gaberdine trousers, dark blue turtleneck sweater and checked tweed jacket. The brim of his faded cloth hat was turned down all around and he held a pipe clenched between his teeth. The woman was much shorter. Her hair was almost white and she wore a skirt and sweater. She walked slowly, using a cane. The two of them were holding hands.

They were coming towards her.

"Carla? But it couldn't be anyone else!" the woman exclaimed in English. She stood peering into Carla's face, not saying anything. Her gaze was intense. She was not quite smiling. Actually, with her small bright face she did seem a little like Mrs Tiggy-Winkle in Beatrix Potter, much more than Antigone out of an ancient Greek tragedy. Carla suppressed a crazy urge to laugh.

"Welcome to Greece, my child!" the woman said in

Greek. When she spoke Greek her voice was deep and throaty, an uneasy reminder of Ismene's voice. Then she reverted to English. "I am your Aunt Tiggie. This is your Uncle Theo."

"I wasn't sure at first," Carla said. "You don't look like your pictures."

"No one ever does," Theo said.

"I would have known Ismene's child anywhere," Tiggie insisted.

Carla's glance nervously measured the space that stretched between her and them. She understood that Tiggie, whom she had never seen before in her life, expected her to rush into her arms and be embraced. For a moment Carla held herself stiffly. Then she smiled and held out her hand. Tiggie pressed it between both of hers. Then Carla shook hands with Theo. There was a pause.

Lighting his pipe, Theo said, "We can't stand here all evening staring at each other. Where is your luggage?" His English, unlike Tiggie's, was almost perfect.

Carla pointed to the suitcase at her feet.

He stooped to grasp the handle. "Put it down at once, Theo!" Tiggie said. "We can get young Mitsos from the coffee house to carry it."

He made a face. "She thinks I'm an old man, Carla."

"It's just that he's not supposed to carry anything heavy," Tiggie said.

"It doesn't have all that much in it," Carla said. "I can carry it myself."

"I wish both of you would stop fussing," Theo told them. "It's not every day that a young niece comes all the way from America to stay with us."

Carla started to protest, but Tiggie said, "Don't insist. If he wants to show off and carry it for you, I suppose we will have to let him. He'll be feeling sorry for himself tomorrow when his sciatica comes back."

Theo strode off ahead of them with the suitcase. For the

moment he did not look at all like an old man. Tiggie said, "Give me your arm, my child. It rests me when I walk."

"Is it far to the house?"

"Nothing is really far in the village, but I'm not walking at all well today. Still, I couldn't not come to meet your bus. How was the trip?"

"It was all right." Already it seemed like something that had happened a long time ago.

"And your father?"

"He's fine, I guess. He's very busy with his law practice."

The streets of the village were already brushed with darkness. When they moved out of the pool of harsh electric light in the square, it was almost as though they had reached the far end of the world. Many of the houses were shuttered. Some of them, Carla saw, were even in ruins, roofless shells that loomed towards the sky from the cobbled streets. Where had they gone, the people who belonged to them? As they passed an occasional lighted doorway or a shadowed courtyard, she was aware of faces that turned towards her with open curiosity.

Beyond one window she could see a sparsely furnished kitchen. A voice called from it in shrill Greek, "Ah, Kyria Antigone, so your niece finally got here from America. May she live for you!"

"I thank you, Kyria Stavroula."

Behind Kyria Stavroula stood two other female figures in sombre black. "May she live for you!" they echoed.

A few steps after that an elderly man detached himself from a whitewashed wall. "Welcome to the child!" he called. Carla jumped. "And all that way by herself, too!"

"Yes, Barba Kostas," Tiggie said. "And safely enough, as you can see."

As they progressed, other voices called out, welcoming the arrival of Kyria Antigone's niece. Carla's face burned. She was glad of the darkness.

"There's not much further to go," Theo called out. "We're nearly there." She blew out her breath in relief.

A tall woman dressed entirely in black appeared in a doorway. She strode towards them.

"So here she is, at last!"

"Yes, Kyria Dimitra," Tiggie answered.

"You are fortunate. I keep waiting, but no one comes for me." She came closer. She peered into Carla's face. It was as though she were searching to see if it was another face, one that she knew.

Theo said quickly, "She is tired now from her long trip, Dimitra. I will bring her to see you tomorrow."

Kyria Dimitra vanished through the narrow doorway under the spidery balcony of her house.

"She was crying," Carla said. "Why?"

"That is a long story," Tiggie said. "It will have to wait for another time. Now we have reached the house."

She saw only a long high stuccoed stone wall. An old door was set in it. The door was a faded green and at least twice as tall as she was.

Theo produced a huge iron key. He inserted it under a wrought-iron latch. Then he turned the great looped handle. It took both his hands to do it. The hinges of the door creaked.

"It needs oiling," he remarked.

"You've said that every day for months," Tiggie told him. "When?"

"I'll get around to it. Tomorrow, perhaps."

"You've said that, too, every day for months."

"So I have. Well, there is still plenty of time."

The door swung slowly open. A whoosh of fragrance rushed to meet them.

Carla let out a gasp. "A secret garden!"

"A walled garden, you might say," Theo said, "but hardly secret. Nothing ever is in a village like this."

She sniffed at the air.

"Honeysuckle," Theo said. "And rosemary. I clipped the hedges this morning."

She was hardly listening. The pathway before them had brought them to a large paved patio, edged with terracotta urns. Geraniums spilled over their edges. There was a marble table surrounded with wrought-iron chairs. And there, at the side, stood the house itself.

"But," she exclaimed, "it's not at all what I expected!"

"And what did you expect?" asked Tiggie.

"Something low and white, like the island houses on the poster I have in my room. This house is different."

It was square, painted a deep, earth-tinged yellow, with tall windows, grey shutters, and a large balcony with an intricate iron railing that jutted out over the double front doors. She could tell from the window sills that the stone walls were at least two feet thick. The ridged roof was covered with rust-covered red tiles.

Theo said, "It isn't really very special. It's a typical Greek house, built a hundred years ago or so. Many of the houses in the village are much grander. This one, however, is very special for me. It was my grandfather's house."

It took a key almost as large as the one for the garden door to unlock the front door. Then Theo stepped back to allow Tiggie and Carla to go inside ahead of him.

They were in a hall paved with squares of black and white marble. On their right hand was the kitchen. The living room was on the left. The furniture was old and almost shabby. The walls were high, hung with old mirrors in carved gilt frames; portraits of people with severe, unsmiling faces; and old paintings of sailing ships. The lamps cast a yellowish glow on the painted wooden ceiling. There were books everywhere. It was a house that looked as though it had been worn smooth by people's living in it.

Carla moved towards the fireplace. The wide mantel

over it was cluttered with curious ornaments and framed photographs. Among the pictures of people in old-fashioned clothes whose faces she didn't recognise, there was one of a much younger Theo in uniform, and Ismene as a girl standing with a slender Tiggie in what must have been a park in Athens. Beside that, in a leather frame, was Ismene in a cap and gown: her American graduation picture. Then she saw her parents' wedding photograph, and tucked inside the frame was a snapshot of herself taken in front of the obelisk in Central Park. She was wearing a snowsuit. She remembered it. Her father had taken it when she was three, and she was frowning because she had no peanuts left for feeding the squirrels. There was still another picture of her, between her parents in the dining room of their apartment, blowing out the candles of her tenth birthday cake.

Tiggie said, "Wouldn't you like to go upstairs and lie down for a while? You must be feeling what they call jet lag."

"It will hit you soon enough," Theo assured her. "It's seven hours later here."

She was feeling something strange, but she was sure it wasn't jet lag. It was an odd sense of being in a house which Ismene had known before Carla was even born. Then she remembered that Ismene had probably never lived in this house. She had been brought up in Athens. Tiggie and Theo had moved to the village after Ismene had left for America.

"At least, Carla, you must be hungry," Tiggie was saying.

"I ate something on the plane."

"That was hours ago."

"Was it? It doesn't seem like that now."

Tiggie and Theo exchanged a glance. Tiggie said to him in Greek, "The child ought to eat something."

"Can I help?" Carla said.

"You're a guest tonight," Tiggie told her. "Tomorrow you can start being a full member of the household."

"All the same, I'd like to help." Helping would mean that she didn't have to talk.

"Then you can go upstairs and wash your hands and face. Theo will show you where."

When she came out of the bathroom, Theo was standing in a doorway. "I've put your bag in here. This is your room."

There was an iron bed, painted white, with brass knobs and a neat, white counterpane; two elderly straight chairs; a bedside table with a bedlight that looked as though it had once been an oil lamp. There was a marble-topped chest of drawers with a mirror that hung over it from an old silk rope; and a crammed bookcase. "Don't mind the books," Theo said. "You're not expected to read them all. They just keep overflowing from our bedroom."

The shutters were open. The garden spread below her in a faint rustle of leaves. Beyond its wall she caught a glimpse of the quay, a glint of sea and a sparse row of masts.

"Fishing boats," Theo said. "In my grandfather's day you could see a whole forest of masts out there. The harbour was lined end to end with sailing ships. And look! Those lights beyond the port, the highest ones, are the lights of Delphi. Your window looks out on Parnassos."

She stared out at the mountain. She had entered a new world, a world that seemed more than seven hours in time from New York. And yet, from the first moment she had stepped through the green doorway of the garden, it had been as though she had walked into something that she had always known. It was like being enfolded in a kind of embrace, an embrace that did not ask you to give anything back.

Theo said, "That window on Parnassos has been

waiting for you for a long time. It can wait a little longer.
Let's go downstairs now."

Racks lined with old blue-and-white picture plates
covered one wall of the kitchen. Braids of garlic and
bunches of dried herbs hung from iron hooks near the
window. Tiggie, in an apron, was at the counter, breaking
eggs into an earthenware bowl. "I will be finished with
this in a minute," she said. "Just sit down at the table, the
two of you. Talk to her, Theo."

The scrubbed wooden table was set with the blue-and-
white dishes. Carla sat. She assumed it must be her place
because of the glass with the garden flowers that had been
set in front of the place. A little carved rack was fastened
on the wall above it. She could not quite make out the date
cut into its dark wood. In each slot of the rack hung a silver
teaspoon. She counted them. Twelve.

"I made that myself one summer when I was a boy,"
Theo said. "My parents lived in Athens, but I used to
spend all my holidays here."

He got up and moved restlessly around the kitchen.

Tiggie said, "I thought you were going to sit at the table
and keep Carla company."

"Where's my pipe? I can't find it."

"You had it a minute ago."

"Ah, there it is!" He went back to the table. "Now we
can talk." His eyes were very blue and clear. She tried to
imagine what he had looked like when he had carved the
little rack for the spoons. She watched him fill his pipe
from his oilskin pouch. When he lit it, she saw that the
matchbox had a picture of wild flowers on it.

"That soldier with a fixed bayonet, the 21st of April one,
was on the box of matches that the bus driver used," she
said.

"I'm sure it was. I keep an old match box from before the
Colonels' time. Whenever I buy a new one, I merely slip
the part with the matches into the old one." He glanced

over towards Tiggie who was cutting up tomatoes and green peppers for a salad. "Is everything nearly ready?"

"Just about," she said.

"Then we might have a small libation." He got to his feet. "What are you going to have, old girl?"

"Just listen to him, Carla! Old girl, indeed." She untied her apron. "My usual *ouzo*, I think."

"What about you, Carla? Will you join me in a glass of white wine?"

Tiggie gave him a quick look.

"A little wine won't hurt her, Tiggie. In spite of what you might think, she's really quite a grown-up girl."

He got three glasses and carefully filled them. Tiggie's *ouzo* was a clear liquid which turned cloudy when he added water and ice to it. It smelled of liquorice.

They filed outside. He pulled back chairs for Tiggie and Carla, but he remained standing. "Now for the Invocation," he said.

Carla glanced curiously across the table at Tiggie.

"He likes to have a little ceremony at the close of the day," Tiggie explained. "Usually he quotes something from one of his ancient philosophers."

"Not every day," he reminded her. "Only when the occasion calls for it."

"Is it the same quotation every time?"

"Not always."

Theo remained poised on the edge of the patio. "It will have to be something special this evening, since Carla is here and it's her first time. I will just say the old one of Plato's, from the *Phaedo*."

"Not in ancient Greek," Tiggie put in. "Say it in English this time so the child also can understand."

Why did they keep calling her *the child*? And did elderly couples always bicker like that?

Theo cleared his throat. As he said the words, he poured a little of the white wine from his glass onto the ground at his feet.

"'Belovéd Pan and all you other gods that haunt this place, give us beauty of the inward soul, and may the inner and the outer man be at one.'"

Tiggie reached out and touched his arm. "That was just right," she said.

An owl called across the garden. The wine was chilled and not at all sweet and it made Carla feel glowing inside. She watched the stars moving in the sky. There were so many of them in the zodiac, forever multiplying as you watched, each with its own life, its own secret.

"It's time to go inside now," Tiggie said. "The soufflé must be ready."

At the table the jet lag suddenly caught up with Carla. Her eyelids were heavy.

"You don't have to finish your fruit if you don't feel like it," Tiggie told her. "You can go up to bed right away."

The sheets were crisp. She slid between them. They smelled of lemon verbena. Or was it rosemary? She was about to reach out and turn off the lamp when there was a light tap at the door. It opened. Tiggie stood there.

"I came to see if you needed anything."

"I don't think so, thank you."

"You are all right?"

"I'm fine. Only I'm terribly sleepy."

Suddenly she wasn't sleepy any more. She eyed Tiggie. This woman had known her mother all her life. She had held Ismene when she was a baby. She had taken her to buy shoes. She had helped her get ready for school every morning. They had shared little secrets, just as Carla had with Ismene.

Tiggie moved into the room.

"You forgot to close the shutters. Tomorrow the sun will come pouring in on you. I'll close them."

"Oh, don't!" Carla cried. "I can't sleep when it's all dark."

"Neither could Ismene when she was your age."

Tiggie stood there and looked at her. Carla could see her soft face with its frame of white hair. It would have been the most natural thing in the world to lean forward and fling herself into Tiggie's arms. Half of her longed to do that. Instead, she stiffened and turned her face away.

"Shall I turn off the lamp for you?" Tiggie asked in that voice which sounded so much like her mother's.

"Yes. Please."

"Do you want your door open or closed? I always leave ours open."

"Closed, please, if you don't mind."

The light had been switched off. Now she heard the door close. There was the sound of Tiggie's irregular footsteps receding down the hall. From the bed Carla could see the lights on Parnassos, hanging there like a far-off chandelier. Except for the baying of a dog somewhere beyond the village, there was no sound anywhere. She closed her eyes. She felt sleep flowing into her, like an invasion. She let it overwhelm her. She wanted to sleep forever, like the dead.

3   *Awakened by Bells*

She was awakened by the sound of bells.

She rubbed her eyes. The morning sunlight hammered at the window. It streamed across the bed, making everything in the room stand out as sharply as though it had been cut out of cardboard.

The bells persisted.

Instead of the early morning traffic of the city outside her window, there was that scattered chiming. It rang in her head like the striking of hundreds of tuning forks. The brass knobs on the bed glittered like small blazing suns. Then she remembered that she was not in her room in New York. She was in a village in Greece.

She wondered if Ismene had ever slept in that bed. She would have to ask Tiggie. No, she would not ask Tiggie after all. What was the use of knowing? If it had ever been Ismene's bed, she had left no trace of herself behind.

After a while she got up and padded over to the window. She leaned out. The thick stone wall was already warm from the sun. It was not only the church bells that were ringing. Where were the other bells coming from?

The mountain's crest was streaked with snow. Below her, in a cloud of blue and white and mauve flowers, the garden waited. Behind the high wall, she could just see the harbour. Beyond the harbour, across a narrow inlet, stretched a long hill. She could make out a flock of goats and sheep straggling across the bare hillside, the bells at their necks tinkling as they moved away from the village. A man walked among them, followed by a dog. The morning air was clear, and she could hear the high, wandering tune that he piped in a minor key. She leaned further out, the sun toasting her face. Even after the flock had passed out of sight, the bells and the shepherd's thin piping still floated in the air.

Slowly, she pulled on a polo shirt and her corduroy jeans. She shoved her bare feet into her moccasins.

When she went to wash and brush her teeth there was no sound from the other bedroom. What time could it be? Her watch was still on New York time. Tiggie and Theo's door was partly ajar, but Tiggie had said that they always left it open. They must be still sleeping. So she would not have to talk to anyone. She could slip outside by herself and look at the garden, "all in the early pearly" as her father always said their first morning every summer in Vermont when he got up even before Carla and her mother.

She crept downstairs. The kitchen table was already set for breakfast. They were sitting there, fully dressed, speaking in low voices. Tiggie was just stubbing out a cigarette, and Theo was smoking his pipe. Between them stood a vase filled with deep red carnations.

They stopped talking when they saw her.

"I didn't hear you," she said. "I thought no one was up yet."

"We didn't want to wake you," Tiggie said. "Theo and I are rather morning people. We are already on our second cup of coffee. Did you sleep well?"

"I thought I'd sleep forever. The bells woke me."

Theo smiled. "You'll get used to them soon enough. Vassilis and his goats and sheep go out every morning, and in the evening they come back. It makes a frame for the day."

Tiggie said, "Come and have your breakfast."

"I'm not really hungry," she said. "Couldn't I go outside first? I can make my breakfast later. I always fix my own at home."

She ran outside. By the time she came back they would have finished, and she could eat alone.

The garden was full of green smells and it was alive with birds. She wondered if there were any snakes or scorpions, but she plunged in anyway. She went aimlessly along the narrow paths that wound among the trees. In her wake petals from the flowering larkspur showered to the ground like confetti. She had the feeling of being nowhere, lost in space. Yesterday she had been in America. Today she was in Greece. Had Ismene felt as strange on her first morning in America as Carla did here, now?

Perhaps she ought to go out and see the village. But then everyone would stare at her, knowing who she was. They would smile and expect her to smile back.

She went back into the kitchen, where they were still at the table. She slid into her place by the spoon rack. A glass of orange juice stood waiting for her.

They seemed to be expecting her to say something, so she said, "The garden door was open."

"It always is when we're home," Theo said.

"And a good thing, too," Tiggie put in. "I'd have been running out there all morning to open it. We had a positive torrent of visitors."

"So early?"

"They all wanted to see you."

"Oh." Her heart sank. "I didn't hear anything."

"I made sure of that," said Tiggie. "I wanted you to sleep as long as you could." There was a wooden board in front of her with a large golden-crusted loaf of bread on it.

She cut off two slices and put them on Carla's plate.
"There's honey in that yellow pot with a bee for a handle,
and the butter is next to you. I'm making fresh coffee. It
will be ready as soon as you are."

"The bread! It's still warm."

"Kyria Dimitra brought it. She baked it herself."

"Does she bring you fresh bread every morning?"

"Unfortunately, no," Theo said. "This loaf is in honour
of you. Those flowers are also in your honour." He jerked
his chin at the carnations. "Old Barba Kostas brought
those."

She leaned forward and sniffed. They had a sharp smell,
like cloves. She smiled. They were even more fragrant
than the ones that came from the Greek florist on Madison
Avenue.

Theo glanced at her over the gold frames of his Benjamin
Franklin half-moon glasses. "Barba Kostas is worried
about you."

"About me? Why?"

"He thinks you are too thin. He says that you are only
half a portion, so to speak, and that we will have to put a
lot more flesh on you before we can get you married off. I
told him there was still plenty of time before we started
thinking about that. Anyway, you might as well dig into
your breakfast. It will make a good start."

She began to drink her orange juice. It had a different
taste from the orange juice at home. It was not the frozen
kind, but freshly squeezed.

"I hope this will be enough for you," Tiggie was saying.
"It's what we always have: juice and bread and honey and
coffee. Would you like an egg as well?"

"No, thank you. As a matter of fact, I don't usually like
breakfast."

Theo regarded her in astonishment. "Really? It's my
favourite meal."

"How could it be?" she asked. "For one thing, there's

no dessert."

"For me," he went on, "breakfast is the most wonderful meal of the whole day. It always seems to arrive like a miracle."

"A miracle? Breakfast?"

"It's a new start, isn't it? A proof that we have survived another long dark night. Isn't every morning like a gift from the Gods?"

"Theo!" Tiggie warned. "You and your discussions! Let her eat her breakfast in peace. Some people don't like to talk in the morning." She turned to Carla. "Don't listen to him if you don't feel up to it. He's articulate from the moment he wakes up. You may well ask how I have put up with it all these years."

"I was only . . ." Theo began. Then he subsided and sat puffing on his pipe, his blue eyes blinking at them from behind a cloud of smoke.

Kyria Dimitra's bread was the best Carla had ever tasted. The honey was wonderful. "It comes from the slopes of Parnassos," Tiggie said. "Our friend Yorgos the beekeeper brings it." The coffee was hot and very strong. She finished it all.

"How do you feel now?" Theo demanded. "What do you want to do about dessert? I mean the rest of the day?"

"Let the child do what she wants, Theo. It's only her first morning."

"All the more reason, then," he said.

Tiggie said, "Before you came downstairs, Carla, we were sitting here making plans for you."

"Plans?"

"Don't be alarmed. We were merely thinking that it will probably seem a little dull here after your life in New York. The days are full enough for us. We have the garden, our books, our own things to do. But there's not really much here to amuse you. We might organise a trip up to Delphi one of these days. Would you like that?"

Delphi! She might learn the secret that she had been on the brink of discovering yesterday. She might even encounter the Python Lady again.

"Theo has a friend who lives there, a well-known poet. You might like to meet him."

She felt a flicker of excitement. That would be something to tell Honor about. And Mrs Schoenberger would want to hear all about it. "Have I heard of him?"

"Probably not. He writes in Greek. His name is Anghelos Eliou."

She started to say that she had seen books of his at home. Her mother had mentioned him. Then she pressed her lips together.

"Theo," Tiggie said, "why don't you take her out this morning and show her the sights of the village? It won't take long. I will just sit here and smoke a cigarette and wait for you."

"There's one problem," he said. "What are we going to call her?"

There was a warning flash from Tiggie. "Carla is a perfectly good name."

"I agree. But Kyria Dimitra has already asked me what it means. She wants to know what kind of a name is it for someone with a Greek mother. As a name, Carla is all right for anywhere else. But it won't do for Greece, where it doesn't mean anything. The local gods have to be propitiated. After all, she isn't a foreigner. She's half Greek."

Carla said, "But I do have a Greek name."

Tiggie said. "There, Theo, I told you."

"To tell the truth," Carla said, "I never cared for it much. I mean, if it had to be Greek, why couldn't it be something everybody knows, like Daphne, or Penelope? But Ersi!"

"Ersi was your grandmother's name," Tiggie said with a tinge of severity in her voice.

"I know. But it doesn't make any sense in English, does it?"

"You mean to say," Theo asked, "that you don't know what your Greek name means?"

She thought for a moment. "I don't think anyone ever told me. Or if they did, I forgot."

"Actually, it's a beautiful name. *Ersi* means the dew of the morning, the freshness of dawn."

She couldn't help giggling. "I could never live up to that. Maybe you could just call me A.M. for short."

"Or R.F.D.?" he said.

She wrinkled her forehead.

"For Rosy-Fingered Dawn."

"I know. That's Homer, out of the *Odyssey*. We had it last year at school, only in English, of course. '. . . Came the rosy-fingered dawn!'"

"You see?" He smiled. "So today has turned out to be a kind of birthday for you." He pushed back his chair. "Where's my pipe, my outdoors one?"

"Exactly where you left it last night," Tiggie said.

"Oh. So it is." He was already in the hall, taking his blue sailcloth hat off its hook. He stood in the kitchen doorway. "Are you ready, Miss Rosy Fingers?"

She threw a quick glance at the dishes on the table.

"Never mind about them," Tiggie told her. "I have my own system. It only takes two minutes, so just go along with Theo. He loves showing off the village. After all, his grandfather was the mayor."

"First, we have to see Hephaistos about something," Theo said.

"I know that name," Carla said. "Wasn't he one of the ancient gods?"

"The god of the fire and the forge, the Greek Vulcan," Tiggie said. "It's what Theo calls Savvas, the local blacksmith and handyman."

"Let me tell you about him," Theo began. "Savvas went off to Athens one day. When he came back he brought a wife from the city, a beautiful young woman.

She was a hairdresser."

"Theo!"

"What?"

"I don't really think it's the kind of story to tell the child."

"Why not? Everybody in the village knows it, so she's bound to hear it sooner or later. Well, she set up shop in his house. And one morning, when he came home unexpectedly, instead of giving a shampoo and a set in the front room, she was in their bedroom with a soldier. They were much too busy with each other to notice Savvas. So what he did was to lock the house and take the key with him. He went back to his workshop and brought back a set of iron bars with him. He blocked the bedroom window with them. Then he shouted to the whole village to come and see. She had to leave on the first bus the next day. The village was still laughing. It was like the time when Hephaistos found his wife Aphrodite in the arms of Ares, the god of war, and trapped them in a net for all the other gods to see."

"Don't start that game now," Tiggie said. "It's too early in the day."

"Is it?"

"Yes, it is. You and your passion for mythology! Anyway, what do you want Savvas for this morning? He told me he couldn't get around to fixing the grape arbour until after Easter."

"I'm not going about the grape arbour. It's something for her."

"For me? Oh, what?"

He looked mysterious. "Let us just say that it is a kind of birthday present."

Tiggie knitted her eyebrows at him. They were thick and still almost black, despite the fact that her hair had gone white.

"Why not?" Theo said. "It's her first morning in Greece,

and she has a lovely Greek name that she has never used before. All that calls for a birthday present."

"Well, Ersi, you mustn't let him wear you out with his stories about the people in the village."

Ersi! So she *was* going to be Ersi now, at least for her time in Greece. It was like a real birthday, after all, her Greek birthday. She would have to write down the date in a book so that she would remember it. She already felt lighter, like somebody who has just blown out the candles on a cake and made a wish. But she was still not sure what her wish was.

Tiggie, cigarette in hand, regarded her oddly. Was something wrong? On that first day in the village maybe she ought not to be going out in wrinkled pants, faded polo shirt and scuffed moccasins. Everything Tiggie had on was immaculate, in soft colours that suited her, and her hair was in perfect order. Her own hair was in such a tangle! She scraped at it with her fingers.

Suddenly Tiggie's face softened. "Have a good time," she called, and waved them out of the house.

4   Time and Thyme

She trailed Theo along the flagged path. He kept stopping
to yank a weed out of the border, or to pinch off a dried
geranium, or to loosen a tangled branch. At one moment
he crouched over a clump of spade-like leaves. "It's
coming along at last," he said. "It's a rare species of
amaryllis. Someone brought Tiggie the bulb from South
Africa, and it's due to flower this summer. Too bad you
won't be here to see it bloom." He pointed to two thick,
gnarled tree trunks, their branches covered with a pale
wash of new leaves. "You won't see the pomegranates,
either, when they get ripe in the fall."

"I've only seen pomegranates in fruit stores," she said,
"never on a real tree. And what's that hedge with the tiny
flowers?" The air was pungent with it.

"That's the rosemary I clipped yesterday." He pointed
to a thick tangle of lacy leaves at their feet. "Run your
hands over that and then smell them."

"It's like the main floor at Lord and Taylor's. There's a
pink soap they sell."

"It's rose geranium. Now try the bush next to it."

"Cologne!"

"That's lemon verbena. You'll find mint and marjoram
in that patch by the patio. It's still too early for basil."

As she surveyed the garden, it ceased to be a green blur

and took on a pattern: olive trees with their shimmering, silvery shade; flowering vines trained against the ochre walls; spiky larkspur that covered the ground with a pastel cloud. "This garden is really like a part of the house," she said, "like an outdoor room!"

The pistachio-coloured door creaked on its hinges and they went through it.

Kyria Dimitra's door was padlocked. "She must have gone off to church," Theo said. "Everyone is starting to get ready for Easter. It's next week."

Further on, an old woman stood in her window, shapeless in her rusty black, her grey hair streaming around her wrinkled face. She came running out into the street, thrusting an old clock into Theo's hands.

"What's the matter this time, Kyria Stavroula? Has it stopped?"

"Our clock never stops. It's the bell. It doesn't ring when it's supposed to."

He put on his half-moon glasses, rewound the alarm and handed the timepiece back to her. "It should ring now."

Clutching it to her chest, she fixed Carla with glittering eyes. Only she wasn't Carla any more. She was Ersi. "You have a new tree in your garden," Stavroula said to Theo in a high-pitched cackle. "May she grow to be a comfort and shade for you and for Kyria Antigone!" After that she scooted inside.

Ersi could see the room through the uncurtained windows. Except for a calendar hanging from a nail, the walls were bare. The furniture consisted of three old kitchen chairs and a wooden table on which the clock ticked away loudly. Stavroula and one of her big sisters had already settled themselves at the window, bending over little cushions set on their laps. Their hands flew among a maze of pins and bobbins, as though their fingers had eyes.

"They are tatting," Theo said. "They make lace all day long. There's not much that passes that they don't see. I call them the Aunts."

"Who knows, my girl," Stavroula called out. "One of these days we may be making the trimming for the pillows of your marriage bed."

The third sister sat outside, on the edge of the whitewashed kerbstone.

"What's wrong, Toula?" Theo asked.

She rolled her faded eyes and pointed to her jaw. "Toothache!"

"What toothache?" Stavroula screamed through the window without interrupting the flying movements of her fingers. "There are no teeth left in her mouth."

"Bite your tongue!" Toula screamed back at her. "If I had teeth they would be aching."

"Don't listen to her. She is only complaining because she is too lazy to work."

"Too lazy, am I? They won't let me!"

"Be quiet. Don't I let you hold the scissors so that you can cut the thread? It's all you're good for. Snip, snip!"

Then she noticed the boy. He had paused by the corner and stood watching them. He was as dark as a gypsy, dressed in a faded shirt and shorts. A flower stuck out of his shirt pocket. When he saw her glance directed at him he darted away like a lizard and disappeared between two walls.

Theo and Ersi moved on. In the narrow back lanes there were donkey droppings stamped onto the cobbles like so many gold coins. A special smell hung in the air. She sniffed, trying to make out what it was.

"Thyme," Theo said. "It's even stronger out on the hillsides. It grows everywhere."

Deserted houses stood on either side, their margins rank with weeds.

There were also archways through which she could

glimpse courtyards with lemon trees, and old olive tins overflowing with geraniums. Laundry hung from lines and scoured cooking pots had been left out in the sun to dry. She heard voices whispering, voices shouting. Faces appeared in the windows to watch them as they passed.

They reached an open door. Inside, a burly figure bent over a bar of iron. Sparks sprayed up at his isinglass mask. The noise from his welder was deafening. "The cavern of Hephaistos!" Theo shouted in her ear.

Savvas switched off the electric welder, shoved the mask back off his face, and peered at them. Small, shrewd eyes blinked at her out of his unshaven face. She looked away.

"That's the girl, is it?"

Theo nodded.

Savvas remained silent.

"Well?" Theo said.

"It's not ready yet."

"When will it be?"

Savvas seemed to be measuring her, memorising her. "I'll bring it when it's right." He pulled the mask back down and turned his back on them, crouching over the fierce blue light of his acetylene torch. Sparks spluttered through the workshop.

Theo shrugged. "He takes his own good time."

"Whatever it is," she said, "it will be a surprise when it comes."

They went back into the daylight. Theo said they might as well take the main street now. "You will want to send your father a card to let him know you got here safely. After that we can go down to the harbour." As they proceeded along the main street, the shopkeepers watching them from the open doorways, Theo said, "You mustn't mind all the attention. There will be a lot of it at first."

"I hate being stared at!"

He looked thoughtful. "Let me explain something. We Greeks are children of the Mediterranean. We live by the sun and by our senses. We cannot exist without sight and without sound. We have to feel everything: with our hands, with our eyes, with our voices. How can we be sure that you really exist until we have touched you?"

She brought two postcards with views of the village, one for her father and one for Honor. As she wrote on them, the postmaster gasped and crossed himself three times.

Theo said, "Apostolos has never seen anyone write left-handed before."

This time she merely glanced at Apostolos and smiled. His amazement was less disconcerting than the searching stare of Savvas, or the Aunts' shrieking. Perhaps she was getting used to being looked at.

As she licked the stamps and stuck them on the cards, she thought, "I'm missing the exams at school!" Then she wondered about her father. How was he getting on, alone in the apartment, without her? She could see him putting a TV dinner in the oven and then settling down with a pile of papers from his briefcase.

Then they were out on the quay with its line of tied-up fishing boats. Just after they turned the corner there was a small *taverna* with tables and chairs set out under a sun-bleached awning. Two old men in stained white jackets sat outside, puffing on cigarettes.

"In the village they call them Bread and Salt," Theo said. "Their real names are Andreas and Petros."

Andreas looked up from the potatoes he was peeling. "Come and have a little glass with us," he called out, "to welcome the girl to the village!"

"It's too early in the day," Theo called back. "Some other time."

At that moment a plump, grey-bearded figure came sailing towards them along the quay. He had on a black robe with full sleeves and a tall black hat like a stovepipe under which his long grey hair was gathered in a neat bun. He held up a black umbrella between himself and the sun. A silver cross swung on his chest. It was the *pappas*, the village priest.

"So she has come to us at last! Praise be to the Almighty Creator! What is your name, my child?"

She remembered just in time. "Ersi, Father."

"A Greek name," he pronounced, "although not a Christian one." He rested a puffy white hand on her head. It smelled of soap and church incense. "Lord," he intoned, "bless Thy servant, Ersi!" Then he sailed off, his batwing sleeves billowing in the wind.

She thought of the Greek church Ismene used to take her to. In the past six years they hadn't gone often; only at Easter. Ismene had been furious because the priest hadn't stood up and spoken out against the Colonels. She had even sent him a letter. "The Church ought to have the courage to denounce them!" she had written. Ersi remembered how different the priest in New York had been: beardless, with short hair, and dressed in a black suit with a turned-around collar, like a priest of any other church. He had always spoken to her in perfect English.

She stole a glance at Theo. "I guess that makes it official. It was like a real baptism, almost."

He smiled.

They sat down at a coffee shop. From inside came the sound of cards being slapped onto tables and the clatter of counters on backgammon boards. Some old men sat at the tables around them, like lizards gulping at the sunshine. "I call them the Argonauts. More mythology," Theo said. "They left the village years ago and went overseas in search of the Golden Fleece."

She remembered them from school. Jason had been their leader. "Did they ever find it, the Golden Fleece?"

"It comes to them every month in the form of social security cheques from America."

"Why did they come back?"

"Why does anyone ever come back home? There's a saying that wherever you go, it's dog eat dog, but at least in your own country they bark at you in your own language. What would you like? A Coca Cola? A *gazoza*?"

"*Gazoza*?"

"It's something like soda."

"I'll have that, since it's Greek."

All the men had turned in their direction, calling out their greetings, except for one. He sat by himself at the far edge of the cluster of tables, a book propped in front of him. He flashed them the briefest of glances. Then his eyes flicked back to his book.

"Who's that? Is he an Argonaut, too?"

"No. Solon is from Athens."

"He didn't say hello to you."

"He prefers not to."

"You aren't friends?"

"On the contrary, we like each other very much. As we say in Greek, we breathe the same air."

"Then why?"

"It's not expedient in these days."

"These days?"

"These days of the Colonels' regime. To them, Solon is a dangerous man. He is an upholder of the Constitution, a judge."

She stared furtively at Solon. She liked his face. It was grave and gaunt, with sparse grey hair above a high forehead. Why was he alone, sitting so far from the other tables? It was as though he were in a kind of quarantine.

"Here you are!" The proprietor had arrived. He set down a cup of thick Turkish coffee for Theo and a bottle with a straw stuck in it. The *gazoza* was cold and bubbly, with a faint taste of lemon. When Theo reached into his pocket to pay, the proprietor said it had already been taken care of. He jerked his head towards the next table where a man in a ventilated baseball cap sat reading a newspaper.

Theo held up his coffee cup. "Your health, Demos!" he called out.

At one moment she saw that dark boy again, the one with a flower in his pocket, loitering at a discreet distance from their table. Was he trying to overhear what they were saying? When she looked again, he was gone.

Theo pushed back his chair and got to his feet. "Enough for one morning," he said. "Tiggie will be waiting."

As they left, she turned in Solon's direction. He raised his eyes. Then he looked away, so quickly that she was not sure whether she had actually seen a flicker of greeting there.

Kyria Dimitra waited for them in her doorway. Without a word she seized Ersi's hands and drew her towards her, engulfing her in a fierce embrace. When she finally released her, Dimitra cried, "Does the child speak Greek? Or did those barbarians on the other side of the world never teach her the language of her mother?"

"I can speak a little Greek," Ersi managed to say.

"Ah, my treasure! The golden child! She is like one of us, after all!" She pressed Ersi's face between her rough hands and covered it with kisses. Ersi stood there stiffly, her cheeks wet with Dimitra's tears.

Still clutching her, Dimitra drew them into the house.

It shone like a silver spoon. The walls were whitewashed, the floorboards scrubbed until they looked bleached. The windows were hung with starched white curtains. Ersi's eyes were drawn to the photograph of a young girl, framed and set out on a shelf in a corner of the room, beside an ikon of the Holy Mother. In front of it hung a small glass lamp filled with oil. A tiny flame floated inside it. Dimitra made them sit at the table in the middle of the room where a tray was set out, spread with an embroidered cloth. On it stood glasses of water and tiny cut glass plates with spoonfuls of jam the colour of garnets.

"We can stay only a moment," Theo said. "Her aunt is waiting."

"And I? Haven't I been waiting?"

She stood over them and watched while Ersi ate the wild cherry preserves and drank the water.

At last they were outside again, leaving Dimitra in the courtyard. Her courtyard was lined with flowers in pots. It was as clean and as shining as the inside of the house.

Ersi waited for Theo to say something. He only lit his pipe and pulled on it.

"You said you would tell me about Dimitra," she said. "Why does she act like that?"

"There's not all that much to tell. Dimitra is a widow. Her husband left to go overseas, like the other Argonauts. He never came back. He left her with an only child, a daughter.

"One day a stranger arrived here. He was handsome, all in black, with a dark, striking face. Word flew that he was rich. His house was like a palace. He owned a whole fleet of shining black automobiles. Someone who had relatives in Australia said that he owned a large undertaking establishment in Melbourne. The moment he saw Kyria Dimitra's daughter he fell in love. Wherever she went, her eyes modestly lowered to the ground as she walked along the lanes to the village, there he was, pursuing her with his dark gaze.

"The day after the wedding he carried her off to his own part of the world, to the far Antipodes.

"They said in the village that she was lucky, a girl with no dowry, to have found such a husband. But Dimitra longed for her child. Her daughter wrote for her to come and visit her. But how could Dimitra leave her house, her garden, her flowering pots? And how could she undertake such a journey? She had never travelled as far as Athens.

"Every morning she goes to the post office. Some mornings Apostos will have a longed-for letter with foreign stamps on it. There might even be snapshots inside. But the trouble with faces in photographs is that they do not open their lips to speak.

"That was why she was weeping now," Theo said. "Not for you, but for her own daughter. As they say here, she is waiting for the evening star."

The words seemed to hang in the air. 'Waiting for the evening star . . .'

Later that evening, Theo raised his glass of wine to the darkening sky and recited in a low voice, "'Evening star, you bring all the things which the bright dawn has scattered: you bring the sheep, you bring the goat, you bring the child back to its mother . . .'"

He turned to Ersi. "A Greek poet wrote that over two thousand years ago. Her name was Sappho."

She was not listening. She was thinking of Kyria Dimitra. Instead of standing there like a stone, she might have said something to her. The next time Dimitra kissed her, at least she would not try to turn her face away.

When they got back to the house, the table was set for lunch, Tiggie stubbed out her cigarette.

"Well, what was it like? Did he show you the museum with the figureheads from the old sailing ships? Did you see the famous altar screen in Aghios Nikolas?"

Ersi shook her head.

"But you were gone all morning. What did you show her, then, Theo?"

"Just the village," he said. "And a few people."

Just the village and a few people! Ersi thought. But it had been much more than that.

"And Theo became my godfather," she said.

She and Theo smiled at each other.

5   The Wings of Pegasus

After lunch Tiggie announced that they were all going upstairs to lie down. "It's time for our siesta."

"You mean I have to sleep in the middle of the day?"

"If you can't sleep, you can just lie there and read. The whole village closes down now. If you go outside you'll find all the shops closed and the shutters drawn. You'll get used to it."

She lay stretched out on the top of the bed, fully dressed. The shutters let in thin strips of the midday glare. Silence hung over everything. There wasn't a radio to be heard anywhere. The birds' chatter had stopped in the garden. Even the cats of the village had left off their prowling and yowling.

She closed her eyes. *Carla*: the name already seemed a faraway thing, something that belonged to another life. Then, before she could decide what it felt like to be *Ersi*, she had fallen asleep.

When she woke the birds were squabbling in the olive trees. Downstairs, Tiggie and Theo sat at the marble table in the garden with empty coffee mugs in front of them. Theo was reading a thick book. The hose had been turned on. The smell of rosemary and lemon verbena and rose geranium, rising from the revived bushes, hovered in the air.

"I was just about to send Theo upstairs with a tray," Tiggie said. "You always need something to wake you up after your afternoon nap. Now you can have it here."

The coffee she brought Ersi was thick and slightly bitter. There was a spoon with a curl of preserved orange peel in thick syrup and a glass of cold water. It wasn't so bad having to take a nap in the middle of the day if you could always have a tray like that to help you wake up.

The bell outside the garden door jangled.

"Visitors? At this hour?" Theo laid his book down and went to see who it was. A moment later he called out, "It's for you, Ersi."

Savvas came close behind him. His grimy hands were clamped around the handlebars of a blue bicycle.

"It used to be red when it was mine," Tiggie said. "It's yours now."

So that was the birthday surprise!

The fresh blue paint shone. A wicker basket sat between the handle bars and a new airpump was clamped in place. Above the bell, at the end of a long antenna, quivered a little Greek flag.

"Aren't you going to try it?"

She made a few turns around the patio. "It's perfect!"

Savvas looked as though he had known all along that it would be. "I only had to make a few adjustments. I didn't expect her to be so tall." Theo asked how much they owed him. He shook his head. "With health!" he said gravely. He saluted them, and left.

Ersi's eyes suddenly widened. Savvas had attached tiny wings to the rear fender. They were brass, but they shone as though he had beaten them out of gold. She hadn't thought of giving the bicycle a name. It was not as though it was a living thing, like an animal. But, "I will have to call it Pegasus!" she exclaimed now.

Tiggie gave her an odd look.

"Do you think it's silly?" Ersi asked. "I mean, wasn't

Pegasus the name of the winged horse of the ancient gods?"

"It was also what Ismene used to call that bicycle when it was hers," Tiggie said.

The next morning Tiggie remarked, "I'm afraid there aren't all that many children your age in the village."

She had already noticed that. Except for that dark boy with the flower, there hadn't been anyone she thought she might get to know, and he had such a curious, elusive look to him. In New York, she had Honor. They used to spend their Saturdays traipsing all over the city. They saved up enough from their allowances to have lunch in exotic restaurants, "What will it be this time?", and they would agonise over whether they would eat Chinese, or Indian, or Japanese, or Italian, or Jewish delicatessen, or something they had never tried before. Whenever they went to a Greek place, Honor was impressed when Carla ordered in Greek, but she always said afterwards, "That *moussaka* wasn't nearly as good as when your mother makes it."

Now, looking thoughtful, Tiggie said, "I suppose I will have to arrange something so that you can get to know a few children here. Meanwhile . . . "

Meanwhile, she had Pegasus; and at least no one told her where to go or where not to go. The only stipulation was that she be back in time for meals. So she went everywhere.

After the second day no one in the village turned to stare at her. They all knew who she was. She never passed old Barba Kostas's house without his giving her some flowers from his courtyard. Stavroula and her sisters left off their lace-making to run out into the street, pinching her cheeks and demanding that she wind up their clock. There was Vassilis, the shepherd, barefoot in all weathers, whistling on his wooden pipe as he limped along on his quick, goat-like feet. There were the village women sitting outside their doorways, their backs turned modestly to the street and their eyes fixed on their embroidery or merely staring at nothing. But their faces seemed to light up when she passed.

Even before she reached the coffee house in the main square she could hear the men who gathered there arguing about politics. She looked for that boy, but he wasn't anywhere. Or did he always manage to vanish before she saw him?

Nothing was far in the village. She could go from one end of it to the other in less than half an hour. Still, there was one part that she had never explored. It was where the last houses of the village straggled up a rocky hill. The ground around them was littered with rubble.

Kyria Dimitra's face went blank when Ersi mentioned it. "I have lived in the village all my life," she said, "but I have never set foot in that place. Nobody ever goes there."

"Why not?"

Kyria Dimitra pressed her lips together. "It is not a very nice neighbourhood," she said, and changed the subject.

That was where the Lonely House stood. It was her own name for it. It looked as though it had been set down in the middle of nowhere. She only saw it from a distance. It wasn't even a house, merely an old stonewalled sheep cote, roofed with wavy zinc.

She never saw any sign of habitation around the Lonely House. And yet, once, as she pedalled along the road above it, her eyes were suddenly drawn to two figures making their way along the narrow rocky path that led towards the village. She stopped to see. One of the local policemen was dragging another man along by the sleeve of his coat. As she watched, the man stumbled and nearly fell. The policeman shouted at him. She was too far away to make out the words. She followed them from a distance. When they went past the school building, which had Junta slogans painted on the walls, the policeman raised the flat of his hand. She saw the man flinch, but the policeman merely gave him a push to make him go faster. Then they turned up the street which led to the police station. She caught only a brief glimpse of the man's face. Could it have been Solon?

That evening, in the garden, she turned to Theo. "Tell me about Solon," she asked. "Why is he here in the village?"

Theo regarded her thoughtfully. "I don't know the whole story. As a judge, he was known to be an inflexible supporter of the Constitution, which the Junta had violated by taking over the government without being elected. But the Colonels didn't bother him at first. There was a chance of his being smuggled to Italy, to friends there, but since the authorities didn't interfere with him, he must have felt safe.

"Then, last November, things in Athens tightened again. A policeman was stationed outside his office. One night when he and his wife were out of the house, the police came and searched his apartment. They took away a load of books, books that any civilised person might have had on his shelves.

"The next morning they came to arrest him. There was no trial. They put him in solitary confinement. They threatened to torture him if he didn't confess. There was nothing for him to confess to. Could you condemn a man just for thinking? In the end they sent him here, with orders for the local police to keep a strict eye on him and to report the name of anyone who spoke to him. He has been here ever since."

Before they left the garden that evening, Theo made his libation. She asked him afterwards, "Why do you do it?"

"To placate the gods and to honour them. I believe that the old gods never died. They are still among us. They keep showing up in the guise of mortals."

"Like who, for instance?"

He replied with a smile, "You will have to discover them for yourself."

After that she looked at everyone she encountered, listening to what they said, wondering which one of them might be one of Theo's gods.

"The villagers have their own mythology," Theo told her one day. "They have a nickname for everyone. They even have one for you by now. You are Tiggie's American grandchild."

"What about you? Do they have a name for you?"

"Of course, I am the Englishman, Lord John Bull."

She had to laugh. "And Tiggie?"

Theo shook his head. "They wouldn't dare," he said.

One afternoon she rode her bicycle beyond the pine forest. She returned in the twilight, along the deserted, uneven coast road.

Something was lying in the spiky bushes by the side of the road. She braked and jumped down from the bicycle. It was a dead kitten. Its paws rose stiffly in the air. Green flies crawled over its slack muzzle. She waved the flies away, even though she knew that they would only come swarming back.

Then she was aware that someone was watching her.

She turned. The boy stood on the road leaning against his bicycle, in his faded shirt and shorts. A red flower stuck out of his shirt pocket.

He propped his bicycle against a rock and ran towards her. He knelt beside the dead kitten. "We can't just leave it here," he said, after a moment. "We'll have to bury it."

She shrank back.

Without a word the boy clambered down to the shore. He returned with sand cupped in his hands. He poured it over the tiny corpse and went back for more sand until it was covered. She watched while he found a flat white stone and placed it on top of the grave. Then he drew a stub of black crayon from his pocket. Pressing his lips together, he carefully printed something on the stone's smooth surface: FOR A CAT UNKNOWN.

"That ought to be enough," he said.

"You didn't put a cross," she told him. "Why? Because it's only a cat?"

"I'm not a Christian," he said. "I don't believe in God. If He exists, would He let people suffer and little cats die?" He straightened up. "I know who you are," he said.

"I've seen you before, in the village," she said. "Who are you?"

His eyes were very green, like a cat's, with long spiky lashes. They fixed her with an intent, unwavering gaze.

"I am Lefteris," he said.

6 *Lefteris*

"I followed you today," Lefteris told her. "I wanted to talk to you. Maybe you can tell me what I want to know."

She looked at him, astonished. "What can I tell you?"

He took a deep breath, like someone about to dive. "What it is like, out?"

"Out where?"

"Outside this country." His eyes raked her face. "Is it true that there are libraries you can go to and take home all the books you want to read, and you don't have to pay? Can you learn anything you want? Is it true that in the schools they don't teach you to hate everybody who doesn't think the way the politicians say you have to? Here, the teachers tell you that anybody who thinks in a different way is the enemy." He rushed on. "And I need something. You have to help me with English. I know some now, but it isn't enough. I need always to learn more."

"You could have asked Uncle Theo. He would be glad."

Lefteris shook his head.

"He is very easy to talk to," she assured him. "The hard thing is to get him to stop talking."

He shook his head again. "In this village it's not easy to talk to people."

"How can you say such a thing? They talk to me all the time, even people I don't know."

"It's different for you. You are Kyria Antigone's American grandchild. I don't belong here. I'm from Athens. I am waiting to go to my father and my mother and my sister, who are in England. That is why I must learn English better, so that when I go there I won't be stupid."

"Why can't you join them now?"

He hesitated. "Maybe at any moment now the word will come that I can leave Greece and go to them. They had to leave because of the Colonels."

"What do you mean? Your parents went off and left you here?"

"It wasn't their fault. It happened that way. In her letters my mother is forever saying, 'Lefteris, you have to be patient. You have waited so long, you can wait a little longer. You must understand that it is all very difficult to arrange from here.' She says it is on account of my papers, my passport. Meanwhile, I live with old Marigoula in her little house, and I go to school here."

There was a look of neglect about him: the shabby pants, his bitten nails, his wrinkled clothes. And when he talked he sounded a lot older than he looked.

"Don't you like it?"

He made a grimace, revealing a gap in his mouth like a clown's blacked-out tooth. "The village? I hate it!"

"I meant the school."

"It's a school," he said.

"What about your friends?"

"I don't have any friends here. At school they're only interested in soccer teams and makes of cars. I'm used to it. It's better to stay secret and alone and to trust no one. Anyway, how can you have a friend in this village when Panaghiotis has his eye on you all the time? He's not watching me now, though. I made sure of that."

"Panaghiotis?"

"You don't know about him yet? Panaghiotis is the

village good-for-nothing. He became an important man after the Colonels came. He's the Junta's spy here. I call him the Horse Fly. I'm not the only one he watches. There is Solon."

"I know. The man who sits alone at the coffee house."

"He is from Athens also."

"But you aren't a political exile like Solon, are you?"

"No. They don't exile children, yet. All the same, I am suspect because my family left the country. Everything in Greece is politics. If you are not for the Colonels, you have to be careful. I know they open my mother's letters before I get them. Even so, I will have to march in the parade on the Twenty-first of April. The whole school will have to take part." He fell silent.

"What happened on the Twenty-first of April?" she asked him.

His mouth fell open. "How can you not know? That was when the Junta took over."

"I know that. I mean, what actually *happened*? How could a few army officers take over a whole country?"

"My father used to write for one of the newspapers in Athens. He says the secret is to do it when nobody, not even the leaders of the country, expects it."

What he said after that came out of him like something in a clogged bottle, sometimes in a rush and sometimes the words came slowly, one at a time.

"We were in Athens when it happened. My father was in England then for his newspaper. I went off to school with Marilena, my sister. She is four years older. I was only in first grade. That morning a tank stopped us at the end of the block.

"There was no traffic in the street, not even a taxi. The kiosk on the corner that sells cigarettes and newspapers was locked. A soldier with a bayonet fixed to the end of his rifle stood at the end of the street. Some people from our building had gathered just outside the entrance. Nobody knew what was going on. Somebody said that Mr Dongas on the third floor had been arrested during the night. Marilena started to cry. 'Mr Dongas wasn't a robber or anything. He was only a professor at the University!'

"We went back to our apartment and turned on the radio. All we could get was military marches. The telephone wasn't working. All the telephones in the city were cut off.

"My mother waited for news. The man from the apartment next door reported that five tanks, their barrels pointed, were outside the Parliament Building. There were soldiers all over the place.

"So we went out onto the balcony to see. The streets were full of soldiers and military cars. At first it was exciting, but after a while it got boring. The only interesting part was when the soldiers surrounded a group of boys with long hair. Marilena said they were students from the University. The soldiers yelled at them. They grabbed one boy by the hair and banged his head against a wall.

"Towards the end of the afternoon the radio announced that the Army had seized power in the country. The borders were closed off. Communication with the outside world was stopped. Greece was in the hands of a new master, the Army.

"One of the men from our building said that Athens, the birthplace of democracy, ought to be congratulated. Why? Because it was the scene of the first military takeover in Free Europe since the 1930's.

"Meanwhile, my mother was worried about my father. When would he be able to get home? Greece was cut off from the rest of the world. He was supposed to be back in two days, in time for Marilena's birthday. 'He promised,' Marilena said.

"Well, my father wasn't able to get back in time. In any case, the party was cancelled. Any public gathering was illegal, even if it was only a children's birthday party. You couldn't risk the police arriving. They would arrest everybody, even the man everyone hired to show Bugs Bunny cartoons.

"My mother managed to get word to my father that it was better to stay where he was. We were going to join him there. After that she was out of the house all day long, running from one ministry to another, trying to get the documents to permit us to leave. My father's newspaper wasn't able to help. It had been closed down.

"Meanwhile, things went back to a kind of order. You didn't see tanks on the streets any more and the military curfew was lifted. The airports were open again. You heard stories about new arrests every day and about prisoners being tortured, and things like that; but people had to go on living and working and doing their daily shopping. And we had to go back to school."

Lefteris paused for breath. By then they had settled themselves on a low mound, facing each other.

"The papers my mother waited for never arrived." He took a deep breath. "Then came the day of our school's annual excursion.

"I can still remember every minute of that day.

"To begin with, our mother asked us not to go. She said she had her reasons. Marilena said she didn't care, but I thought I would rather die than not go. I had been looking forward to it ever since I started first grade. Everybody in my class was going, and I had a pair of new hiking books I had been saving to wear. I made such a fuss that in the end my mother gave in. I can still see the look she gave me. 'All right, my Lefteris,' she said, shaking her head, 'but you will come right home as soon as the trip is over.'

"It was a glorious day. Everybody noticed my new boots. We played games. We built a fire by the sea and had a picnic around it. We sang songs. I picked a bunch of wild flowers for my mother.

"When the bus dropped me off in front of our house, I

65

ran upstairs with the flowers. It seemed a little strange to me that it took such a long time before the door was opened. The apartment was quiet. I couldn't hear any voices, not even the radio. And instead of my mother and Marilena, there was only Marigoula, our old housekeeper, standing at the door.

"She didn't smile when she kissed me.

"'What's the matter, Marigoula?' I asked.

"Tears were streaming from her eyes. She put her arms around me and held me very tight. 'Oh, my Lefteris, my golden boy, what is going to become of you now?'

"'What's happened, Marigoula? Where are they?'

"She crossed herself. 'They've gone,' she said.

"'Gone? Where?'

"'To England, to your father.'

"I couldn't believe what she was saying.

"'The papers came today,' Marigoula said. 'The permission was for twenty-four hours and there was only one plane for England. They had to leave. They had to be at the airport by six o'clock. Your poor mother packed everything in a hurry. She even packed a suitcase for you. There it is in the hall. Marilena telephoned my neighbour and I came as soon as I could. They waited for you until the last minute, but in the end they had to go and catch that plane. There was nothing else your mother, poor thing, could do.'

"'What about me? How could they go away and leave me behind?'

"'You will join them as soon as you can.'

"I still couldn't take in what had happened to me. When the plane had left for London I was still picking the flowers.

"From somewhere in her dress Marigoula pulled out a folded sheet of paper. 'Your mother left a letter for you. What does it say? I don't have my glasses.' The truth is that Marigoula doesn't know how to read or write, but she always says it's her glasses.

"I still have that piece of paper. I don't know why I kept

it, because I can remember every word. My mother had printed it in big letters for me to make it out easily. At the end she said, 'You will be coming very soon. I pray that the day will soon come when we will all be able to live in freedom and with nothing to fear, in our own country which we must always love in spite of everything. Always remember that you are as dear to me as my own eyes. I count the days until I see you again. Be a good boy and God will bless you and bring you back to me soon. I kiss you tenderly. Your mother.'

"'She was crying when she wrote it,' Marigoula said.

"When a week passed and my mother sent word to us that my papers were still not ready, that she wasn't sure exactly when they would come, Marigoula said that we would go to her house because my mother had arranged for some journalist to live in our apartment until we came back from England.

"So Marigoula took me home with her. I took the suitcase my mother had packed for me and some of my books. I left my new boots behind. I didn't want them any more.

"We had to take two different buses to get to Marigoula's house. I had never been there before, and I was surprised to see how far she had to travel every time she came to us.

"The next day one of her neighbours came with an old truck. He piled our things in the back and we sat up in front. Suddenly she clapped her hands to her forehead. 'I forgot Vangelis!' she cried.

"She climbed down and came back with an enormous framed picture of her husband who died during the war. She said that Vangelis would have to travel up in front with us.

"He took up so much room that the driver cursed him under his breath every time he had to shift gears. But finally we made it here, to her village, to the little house that had belonged to her godmother. I have been here for six years."

Lefteris left off speaking. The only sound was the lapping of the sea on the shingled beach below them. It was dark by now.

"Six years!" Ersi exclaimed. "Why has it taken so long?"

He picked up a stone and sent it skimming across the water. "Of course I was too small then to understand what had happened. I was angry at them. How could they have done such a thing to me? It was like when someone hits you in the belly when you're not looking for it. At the same time I was afraid because I had been left alone, without them. I was also frightened of my own anger. I mean, how could I be so angry at them when I knew that they loved me? I was all mixed up, angry and being frightened, and loving them, and I didn't know what to feel most." He stared down at the sea at his feet. Then he went on. "But I have had these years to think about it. I suspect sometimes that the Colonels' people must be holding back my papers on purpose, so that my father will have to come back to Greece to get me. Then they will be able to arrest him on account of all the articles he has written in England against the Junta. Anyway, I am still here, still waiting. I try to remember what my mother wrote, that we must love our country in spite of everything. But how can you still go on loving a country where they let such things happen?"

There was a long silence. After a while Lefteris broke it, saying in a low voice, "Would you like to be my friend?"

"Of course," she answered. "But I thought you didn't trust anyone."

"That's true. And you are the first person I have told this to. Would I have told you all that if I didn't trust you?"

"Probably not."

He flashed her a grin, showing the gap in his teeth. "I could tell when I first saw you. You are like me, secret and alone."

It was late. Tiggie and Theo would be waiting. She got to her feet. "When will I see you again?" she asked.

"We could meet here, beyond the pine forest. I will come every day, when I can."

"How will I know?"

"I will be waiting for you. If I get here first, you'll see my bicycle in the bushes. It's better if we come separately."

"Why?"

"The Horse Fly." Lefteris's eyes darted past her, peering down the empty coast road. "The eyes of Panaghiotis are everywhere, even in the back of his head."

He took the red flower from his pocket and placed it on the small cat's grave at their feet. Then he got on his bicycle and was off.

When she reached the village, she tried to see it through Lefteris's eyes: an unfriendly place, a place of exile, in a country where they let such things happen.

7 The Death of a God

The next day, when Ersi came back from the square with Theo's newspaper, Tiggie was waiting for her.

"Theo has gone off to work on his boat. So could you run over to the Nettle and pick up some eggs for me?" The Nettle was what everyone in the village called the man who ran the store nearest the house. He sold fruit and vegetables as well as yoghurt and fresh eggs.

"How many?"

"Three dozen should be enough."

"They ought to make some omelette!"

"What are you talking about? Omelettes! Today is the Thursday before Easter."

Of course, she should have known. Thursday before Easter she had always helped Ismene colour the eggs, but only ten or so, enough to put in a bowl on the dining room table. They were never in soft pastel colours like the dyed eggs everyone else had. Greek Easter eggs were always a deep red.

The Nettle had Tiggie's eggs all ready, along with a small envelope of dye powder. He gave her one of his grudging smiles. "And next year!" he said.

Tiggie boiled the eggs, putting vinegar in along with the dye, "to fix it". After they cooled, Ersi helped her rub each one with a cloth dipped in oil, until it shone. The colour was a deep ox-blood. They glowed in two large bowls. The eggs were not to be touched until after midnight on Saturday when everyone came back from church.

All of Friday the church was shrouded in silence. At one moment she passed the church of Aghios Nikolas. She could see Kyria Dimitra and a group of women inside, all in black. She wondered if Marigoula was one of them. They had brought baskets of flowers with which they were decorating the bier on which the dead Christ would be carried. Ersi stood for a while and watched them. Then she went out beyond the pine forest.

From the books in her room she had picked out some that she thought Lefteris might like: *Treasure Island*, *The Red Pony*, and *The Catcher in the Rye*.

There was no sign of Lefteris. She waited for more than half an hour. In the end she hid them in the bushes, hoping he would find them there when he came.

In the evening the *Epitaphios* took place, the funeral service for the dead Christ.

She stood with Tiggie and Theo on the quay. They waited for the processions of the three churches of the village to converge. A candle burned in every window. The candles were not white, but made of dark brown wax, for mourning. Everyone held a dark candle as well.

It was not long before she could hear the chanting as the processions approached from different directions. The largest procession, the one from Aghios Nikolas, had a brass band. It played Chopin's *Funeral March*, very slowly. After that came the priest; then the catafalque, covered with the flowers that the women had arranged on it, borne along by the church elders in dark suits. On it lay an embroidered representation of Christ's dead body, sewn with gold and silver thread. Behind the bier marched the port authorities, the policemen and the Mayor. A sense of terrible calamity and sorrow hung over everything. The air was heavy with the smoke from the candles mixed with the smell of incense and decaying flowers. Even the small boys who swung the incense burners looked solemn. Some of the women were wiping their eyes. And there was old Dragonas who owned the mini-supermarket on the square. Only the other day she had seen him cheat a foreign lady of ten drachmas. Now he was weeping, his crafty eyes red and filled with tears. She looked for Lefteris, even though she knew that he didn't believe in God.

All the same, she wished he was there, because what they were witnessing was not only the death of a God. It was like the burial of someone that everybody knew. She felt like crying with the others but at the same time something held her back. What was there to weep over? It was only a piece of embroidered cloth.

After the three processions met, everyone straggled off. She and Tiggie and Theo were among the last ones to move silently home through the empty streets.

She went up to bed first. She lay there, the weight of the darkness pressing down on her. After a while she heard Tiggie and Theo coming upstairs.

Would Tiggie stop by her room? Ersi turned her face apprehensively towards the door. Tiggie's uneven footsteps came to a halt outside in the hall.

"Are you still awake?" Tiggie whispered.

"Yes."

"Would you like me to come in and see you? Just for a minute?"

After a moment she answered, "Yes, please."

Tiggie came in and sat on the side of the bed. Ersi moved to make room for her.

"Are you all right?"

"I'm fine."

"Are you sure? I have seen the Good Friday procession every year, so many times, and each time it moves me more than I can say."

Ersi remained silent.

Tiggie said, "You must be thinking about Ismene."

Ersi gulped. Then she burst out suddenly, "It wasn't fair. There was no time. We never even said goodbye when she went out the door. And only the day before that I had yelled at her that my hands were as clean as I could get them without scraping the skin off. And the next thing she was dead. They decided it would be better if I didn't go to the funeral. I didn't even wear black. They don't do that in America. It's not like here. If she had died in Greece, at least I would have worn black for her." She lay there, staring at Tiggie.

"I suppose it helps to wear mourning," Tiggie said. "There is a meaning to it. Sometimes it does you good to show your grief."

"I think about her all the time. I know that she's dead, but I keep forgetting. And then when I come home from school she's not there waiting for me."

"I know. It's hard for me, also, to think that I will never see her again," Tiggie added quietly. "The presence of the dead is imaginary. What is real is their absence."

"The worst part is in the morning, when it's time to go off to school. She always used to go down the hall with me and wait until the elevator came. And I keep seeing that car accident all the time, even though I wasn't there. I close my eyes and try to blot it out, but I can't. Even though it's still not real to me, it won't go away."

"It doesn't help, trying to blot out something that you can't bear," Tiggie said. "The more you try, the more it follows you. The only way to erase pain is by facing it steadily. I knew a wise old doctor, years ago. When I asked him what to do when sorrow comes, he told me, 'Just take it gently by the hand.'"

"I was ready to cry tonight, at the *Epitaphios*. Why? It was nothing but an old banner. And the other day I was almost in tears when there was a little dead cat on the road.

73

But I wasn't even able to cry for my mother. Why? Am I some sort of a monster?"

"I don't think so. Some things you feel are even deeper than tears."

She swallowed. After a moment, she said, "Did you love her a lot? My mother, I mean."

A long silence filled the room before Tiggie answered.

"Ismene was very dear to me, as dear as if she had been my own child. When she went off to America to go to college, I knew that in a way I was losing her, maybe forever. But she wanted to go so much that I had to be happy for her. She was so thrilled over her scholarship." She glanced down at Ersi. "You are almost as old as she was then."

"What was she like? Then?"

Tiggie knitted her dark brows. "It's hard for me to see her as she was then. She was so close to me."

"But how can I ever find out? I want to know everything about her. There are some pictures, old snapshots. I've studied them a million times, but they don't help. And now my father has stuck them away somewhere. You are the only one who can tell me what she was like, then."

"Well, of course she looked very much like you," Tiggie began slowly. "But I think what mattered most to me about Ismene was not so much how she looked, but how she felt. She was always full of passion."

"What kind of passion? About what?"

"About everything: ideas, the world, freedom. She hated injustice. She could never understand unkindness or cruelty. She was forever feeding stray dogs and dragging home sick kittens. She kept wondering what it was like to be an orphan. I would say to her, 'Don't you know?' 'Oh, no!' she would answer. 'I mean a *real* orphan. I have you.' Even though she was so tender-hearted, she was also fierce. Ismene was always ready to fight to the death for what she believed in."

"Do you think I will ever be like her?" Ersi cried. "Really like her?"

"You probably are, more than you think. Now let me smooth out your face. It's all crumpled, like a baby's." She reached out and ran her hand over Ersi's cheeks. "It's late," she said. "We can talk more tomorrow, if you like."

"About her?"

"Why not? But I don't mean only about her, about other things as well. We must have a thousand things to say to each other."

"I don't think I have all that much to say."

"I thought young people talked all the time. Ismene was a positive chatterbox when she was your age."

"Was she?"

"You could tell me about your life in America, or about how you see things in Greece. But now you have to get some sleep. You must be tired."

Ersi sat upright. "You know," she said, "I didn't want to come to Greece at all. Not without Ismene, I mean. But even coming to Greece by myself seemed better than not feeling anything, and sitting through all those movies."

"It doesn't matter how you felt then, does it? The point is that you did come. Theo and I are terribly happy to have you here. First, because you brought Ismene back to us."

"Did I?"

"In a way. Then, after that, because it was you."

Suddenly Ersi stretched out her arms and put them around Tiggie's neck. "I'm glad you came in just now. I wasn't sure that I wanted you to, at first." She breathed in the warm sweet smell of Tiggie's skin. It reminded her of the way her mother used to smell.

"Go to sleep now," Tiggie told her. "Tomorrow is going to be a long day. We will be staying up for the Resurrection."

"I don't think I can fall asleep now."

"You will, if you lie perfectly still and try not to think."

"That's the hardest thing of all."

Tiggie was smiling at her through the milky moonlight. "It's even worse when you have nothing to think about." She smoothed the bedcover. "I always used to do this for Ismene."

"Did you always leave the door open a little?"

"Sometimes." She bent down and kissed her on the cheek. When she went out of the room she left the door open, just a stripe of light. The smell of Tiggie's skin, so like Ismene's, lingered on Ersi's cheek.

8   *The Inseparable Enemies*

The flowers of Lazarus were all over the village. They grew rife wherever you looked: bright yellow daisies with feathery leaves, exploding like masses of sunlight all over the fields, out of the rubble of fallen walls, spilling out into the lanes. They seemed to be as much a part of Greek Easter as the blood-red eggs.

Saturday, the day after the *Epitaphios*, the air was charged with expectation, like a current of electricity. Ersi did not know what to do with herself. Theo had gone off to see some friends. Ersi wanted to help Tiggie, who had a lot to do in the kitchen, but in the end she felt more like a nuisance than a help. Everyone else was involved in preparations for Easter. Kyria Dimitra's door was closed. The taverna was shut down. The coffee houses were empty. Stavroula and her sisters sat on their doorsill with their hands folded. They didn't call out to her to wind their clock. Time had stopped for them that day.

She went back to the house. Tiggie sat in the kitchen with a book, smoking a cigarette as she read. Theo was still out.

Tiggie laid down her book. "Well? What was happening?"

"Nothing."

"Then come and talk to me. Tell me about Easter in

New York."

"Easter in New York? Ismene used to take me to the Greek church on Sundays until the Colonels came into power, but so many of the Greeks there were in favour of them that she stopped going. After that we only went for the Resurrection."

"Didn't you find that exciting? I always do."

She thought about it. For one thing, Greek Easter hardly ever fell on the same day as everybody else's; and for most of her friends, like Honor, Easter meant new clothes and the Fifth Avenue parade and bunnies and baskets filled with jelly eggs and all sorts of things they didn't have in the Greek church. For her, it was almost like being Jewish and celebrating Passover. She said, "It always seemed, well, *foreign*, if you know what I mean."

She felt restless. She went outside again. When she turned the corner, there was a small dark figure leaning in the shadow of the wall, a sprig of Lazarus daisies sticking out of his shirt pocket.

"Lefteris! I looked for you yesterday."

"Marigoula needed me."

"Anyway, I left some books for you."

"English books?" His eyes lit up. "Where?"

"In the bushes, where you put your bicycle."

"I was there today. I didn't see any books."

"Perhaps you didn't look very hard. After all, you weren't expecting them to be there."

His eyes had taken on a guarded, thoughtful look. "You shouldn't have done that," he said.

"Why not?"

"There could be consequences."

"Consequences? Over three paperback books in English? I think you must be exaggerating things a little bit. And why are you waiting out here in the street? Why didn't you come to the house?"

From his expression she understood that he would have

liked to, but he shook his head. "Maybe your uncle and aunt wouldn't think I was a good friend for you to have."

"That's crazy. I'm sure they'd like to know you."

Lefteris did not answer.

"Do you want me to meet you at the pine forest, then?" she asked.

"No," he said quickly. "I'll go by myself. I have to find out what happened to those books. Anyway," he added, "I can't stay out much longer. Marigoula wants me to whitewash the steps outside the house for Easter. She says she doesn't have the strength to do it herself this year."

"Then maybe we could just go for a little walk in the village."

"Maybe."

"Why maybe?"

"Well, there are the others."

"What others?"

He lowered his eyes. "The other children. If they saw you with me they would point and laugh and whisper to each other."

Was Lefteris exaggerating again? Maybe everything he told her was a little bit exaggerated.

"And then," he went on, "there is Panaghiotis. I am not saying this because of me, but for you."

"I never heard anything so ridiculous! Who is Panaghiotis to tell me who my friends are?"

In the end, Lefteris agreed to go for a very short walk, although he still looked dubious.

There seemed to be a lot of people in the village that she had never seen before. Houses which had been shuttered were open now, and cars with Athens number plates were parked outside. "They belong to families who live in the capital now, or in Piraeus," Lefteris explained. "They have returned to celebrate Easter in their village." Most of the men wore suits and ties. Their wives had on city dresses and they tottered along the cobble-stoned lanes in tight new high-heeled shoes, greeting each other.

"Just look at them!" Lefteris said. "They think they are better than the villagers who remained behind."

One thing she tried not to see: the newly slaughtered lambs hanging outside the butcher shops. Only the day before they had been bleating in the wake of Vassilis's music, cropping clovers from between the stones out on the hills and trotting along on delicate hooves, leaving their droppings strewn on the paths like little black marbles. "I won't eat even the smallest bit of roast lamb tomorrow," Lefteris told her. "I won't either," she vowed.

They climbed along the back lanes until they came to a spot where the houses ended. From there they could see the whole village, spread out below them like a panoramic postcard. Lefteris pointed to the spit of land opposite the harbour. "It wasn't always a pine forest," he told her. "In the old days, in the time of the sailing ships, that was where the shipyards were. All the tall cedars that grew there were cut down to make masts."

"For someone who says that he hates the village," she said, "you seem to know a lot about it. Do you know about the village's mythology?"

He frowned. "What mythology?"

So she told him about Theo's mythology game.

For a moment his face lit up. Then he shook his head. "There are no gods in Greece any more. Maybe they came down from Parnassos a long time ago. But now everyone is like Kyria Rinió and Kyria Katya."

"Like who?"

"Let me tell you about them. They live just beyond Marigoula's house. I see them every day. Each of them sits on a wooden chair in front of her own doorway. A plum tree grows in Rinió's courtyard. Its branches stretch out to shade the street. But if a leaf flutters to the ground, Katya gets very angry. She sweeps it right over to Rinió's side.

"Every Monday morning there is the great laundry race. Which of them will get hers out on the line first? Marigoula says that Rinió always has a nightgown or an apron already rinsed out from the night before, so that the minute she gets out of bed she can peg it outside for all the neighbourhood to see. The rest of her washing comes later. But she is always the first.

"Then there is Katya's fig tree. It used to spread out over the garden wall that divides their two houses. One summer Rinió rented a room in her house to a couple from Athens. Katya overheard her telling them that they could eat as many figs as they liked from her side of the wall. There were so many that year, and it was a pity to let the birds and the wasps get them all. She couldn't eat them herself because of her diabetes.

"That was all Katya needed to hear. She went and heated a big kettle of water. When it was boiling she poured it over the roots of the tree. It killed the tree, but she was satisfied. She wasn't going to have Rinió offering her figs to anyone who wanted them.

"Now, whenever I see Katya sitting outside her house with her soft face and her grey hair in its tidy bun, I wonder how she could have murdered her own fig tree.

"Rinió and Katya have lived side by side all their lives. Their children have grown up and left the village. Each of them is all alone in the world. Each eats all her meals alone. Every day and all day long they sit a few feet apart, each in front of her own door. They do not speak to each other. In the village they call them 'The Inseparable Enemies'."

Lefteris stared ahead of him at the village spread out beyond their feet. "It may be mythology to your uncle Theo," he said at last. "To me it is like everything else that I see in Greece. We live side by side and yet we cannot live together. We are like inseparable enemies. Do you have people like Panaghiotis and tree-killers in America?" His green eyes searched hers. Then he got to his feet. "I have to go now."

"I could go with you and help you whitewash," she said.

He shook his head. "There's only one brush. Anyway, I have something else to do first."

"What?"

He grinned. "I'm going into the mouth of the wolf. I want to find out what happened to those books."

He was already on his way, in the direction of the pine forest. She couldn't help smiling as she watched him bound along the uneven path in his old sandals, moving like a cat, ready to face Panaghiotis, the villagers, the whole world.

A moment later Lefteris was out of sight. There was only the little sprig of yellow daisies, the flower of Lazarus, that he had left behind for her on the low stone where they had been sitting.

When she got to her feet she noticed a girl further down on the path, watching her.

"Oh, hello!" Ersi said. But the girl walked away very quickly without a word.

9 *A God Rises*

They had to get to church around ten that night so that Tiggie could find a seat.

When it was time to get ready, nothing that Ersi had brought with her seemed suitable. Her New York dresses were too hot. Her skirt and blouse were wrinkled. She gave an angry twitch to her cardigan. It looked so dreary. What did you do when you no longer had a mother to tell you what to wear with what and how to fix yourself up?

Tiggie appeared. "I came to see how you were getting on."

"I'm not sure. Just look at me! Am I all right?"

"For one thing, you might do something about your hair."

"I know." She scraped impatiently at it with her fingers. It hung around her neck in uneven lengths. "You don't approve of it this way, do you?"

"You have pretty hair. It's like Ismene's."

"I suppose so. But I mean, do you like it this short?"

Tiggie regarded the irregular spikes as though noticing them for the first time. "I thought that must be the style in New York this year, so I didn't say anything."

"How would you like me to wear it?"

"Longer, I think, would suit you better."

"How much longer?"

Tiggie smiled. "Does it matter what I think?"

"Yes, it does."

Tiggie judiciously cocked her head to one side. "Well . . ."

"It used to be nearly to my shoulders. I hacked it all off in the kitchen with a bread knife the day Ismene died."

"Did you? Why?"

"Because she loved it so."

"I should think you might have wanted to keep it, then, for her sake."

"Really? You know, I never thought of that."

"And you could brush it more often, to make it shine."

"To tell the truth," she said, her cheeks reddening, "I didn't think it mattered to anyone any more how I wore it and if I brushed it or not."

"Not even to your father?"

"He never notices anything like that."

"Are you sure?" Then Tiggie added mildly, "Anyway, if I were you, I would just let it grow out. Would you like me to brush it for you now?"

"Would you? I'm afraid my brush isn't awfully clean."

"I've seen worse. Now stand still."

She stood there, not moving, while Tiggie brushed out her hair. It was a soothing feeling, being looked after, being cared for again.

When Tiggie finished, she said, "Wait here for a moment." She came back with a blue velvet ribbon and a large square of printed silk. She tied the ribbon around Ersi's hair. "That's better," she remarked. She handed her the scarf. It had a design in green and blue. "Try this around your shoulders."

"But . . ."

"Don't you like it?"

"Oh, yes. It's perfectly lovely, like all your things."

"It's from Hermès, in Paris. I've never worn it. I thought it might be too young for me. It's just right for you, though. It's yours, now."

"Really? Oh, Tiggie!"

"Consider it my Easter present. You have to put on something new for Easter."

"How should I wear it? I never learned how to tie a scarf right."

Tiggie's fingers deftly arranged it around her shoulders, with a loose knot at the side. She shoved her in front of the mirror. "Look at yourself."

She looked changed. She turned back to Tiggie. "But weren't you going to wear this scarf yourself?"

Tiggie shrugged. "I hadn't really made up my mind about it."

"But now you don't have anything new to wear."

"It doesn't seem all that important any more," Tiggie said. "Not at my age."

This time they carried white candles, tall slender ones. Theo had stuck them through little plastic cups which would catch the dripping tallow after they were lighted.

Ersi had assumed that they would be going to the big church, to Aghios Nikolas. Instead they were going to Aghios Ioannis, the oldest and the poorest church of the village.

It was already filling up when they got there. The service had begun. There were two empty seats in the women's section. Theo stood against the wall on the right hand side of the church, with the men. Ersi looked around. Everyone was in bright new clothes. She was grateful for Tiggie's ribbon and scarf. At first glance she did not recognise most of the people she saw. The women's heads had emerged from the curlers and kerchiefs they had worn all day. As for the men, they were spruced up in their unfamiliar good suits. They wore ties. Their shoes had been polished to a high shine that reflected the bright electric bulbs of the chandelier. The Nettle's son, home from sea, had on a velvet jacket, red as a dyed egg. There was no sign of

Lefteris. Everyone held a candle in readiness for the great moment, the Resurrection at midnight.

Tiggie nudged her. She turned her attention to the service. The air was heavy with incense. The gold backgrounds of the ikons gleamed. The royal doors of the altar screen were open, and the priest had come out to stand between them. Instead of wearing his everyday black robes and rusty stovepipe hat, he was enveloped in a garment that was all brocade and cloth-of-gold. His long hair, loosened from its usual tight bun, streamed down over his shoulders. The white hairs in his beard glistened. It was as though he had stepped out of one of the ikons on the royal doors. His voice was raised in a chant. Nearby, the cantor stood at a lectern, chanting in his turn. Now and again they would both pause for the congregation to intone the responses.

Theo had observed earlier that the liturgy of the Church was like a performance of grand opera, only without an orchestra. She understood now what he meant. The priest stood in front of the altar as though he were in the centre of the stage, singing an elaborate aria. Then the cantor took over. The people in the church were the chorus. The women all around her held books, but they didn't need them. They knew the words by heart. The words were in old Greek, not the kind of Greek that everybody spoke nowadays.

"What are they saying now?" she asked Tiggie in a whisper, just as she had always asked Ismene; and Tiggie said, "It's from St. Mark's Gospel."

She gave up trying to follow the words. She let herself float in them. By now people had begun to glance at their watches. It was nearly midnight. There was a surge of expectation, followed by a restless silence. The children up in the balcony were hushed.

The priest stood before the altar. In his hand he held a candle which had been lit from the holy flame on the altar.

His voice rose as he read the words of the angel who appeared to the three Marys who had come to the tomb to find the body of the crucified Christ. "'He is risen,'" he chanted. "'He is not here. Behold the place where they laid Him . . .'"

Then, one by one, all the lights in the church were being dimmed. The church became as dark as the sepulchre itself. The priest moved slowly towards the door of the church, followed by his acolytes and the cantor. "Come now and receive the light!" he sang out.

A long sigh surged through the church. Then everyone pressed forward, stretching out candles to be lighted from the priest's. Ersi noticed one of the boys who swung a silver incense burner in front of the priest, his blue jeans nearly concealed by his long white robe. His slicked-back hair had been brushed until it was like an animal's fur. His face was scrubbed pink. His eyes were filled with the solemnity of the moment and his own importance in it. Suddenly she realised that it was Mitsos, the boy from the coffee house in the square. Usually she saw him tearing around on his motor bike, grimy and scruffy, a cigarette clinging from the corner of his mouth. When he saw her, his expression of holiness did not change. All he did was to blow a large bubble of pink gum at her.

Now the sacred flame, the light from the altar, the light from the sepulchre, travelled from candle to candle. Everyone was pressing outside towards the courtyard of the church. She and Tiggie moved with the others within a spreading sea of light. Theo came and stood beside them. She and Tiggie lit their candles from his. "Christ is risen!" he said.

The three of them kissed each other. "Truly He is risen!" The shouts rose all around them. "He is risen! Truly He is risen!" By now the bells in the belfry filled the night with frantic jangling. Shots rang out, so loudly that they might have been cannons being fired off.

"Aaaaaaaah!" the crowd sighed. The first rocket had gone up. It spread across the sky, a burst of golden joy.

Now from the village's other churches, and last of all from the tiny Church of Our Lady of Everlasting Tenderness, which was not much bigger than a chicken coop, they could hear the bells ringing out and the guns being fired.

From high up in the bell tower of Aghios Ioannis she could hear the boys shouting in triumph, "We were the first this year!"

A woman shrieked. There was a moment of panic. Someone had set off a string of firecrackers. They spluttered wildly, zigzagging all over the pavement. The sky was filled with rockets. Outside the church, all the faces glowed, lit by candle flames. Everyone was kissing someone and being kissed in turn, crying out joyfully, "He is risen! Truly He is risen!" The bells went on clamouring in Ersi's ears.

They held their lighted candles in their cupped hands as they walked home. If your candle went out, you could not relight it from a match or a cigarette-lighter. You had to take the flame from someone else's. On the way villagers stopped to greet them, smiling.

"Christ is risen!"

"Yes, truly He is risen!"

In New York you went home from the Greek church in a taxi, sitting inside and shielding your candle. You had to ask the driver if he wouldn't mind rolling up his window, so that it wouldn't blow out. The people in the street, going home with their newspapers after a Saturday night out, stared at you and wondered what was going on.

Ersi found herself looking around her now, half-expecting to see a face that had always been beside her at every other Easter of her life. For a moment she thought that she had caught a glimpse of it, but it was only Tiggie's face, looking younger in the glow of her candle. Tiggie glanced questioningly at her. Her lips moved, but Ersi could not hear what she said.

And, after all, did it matter what Tiggie was trying to tell her? Because suddenly she knew that Christ was truly risen this time. The whole village, all of Greece, was filled with the holy light that they were bringing home with them.

A light supper was always part of returning from church after the Resurrection. A loaf of sweet bread that Tiggie had baked stood on a silver dish, a red egg embedded in its glazed braided crust. She had prepared the same special soup made of lambs' liver and lights, and herbs – mostly dill – that Ismene had always made. They stuck the candles in a tall glass on the sideboard.

Then it was time for the game with the eggs.

You had to choose one, and the idea was to see whose was the strongest. Theo held his egg out while Ersi banged hers down on it as hard as she could, at each end. Both times the shell of her egg cracked. It was Tiggie's turn to take on the winner. She held her egg with its pointed end downward. With a quick, deft movement, she barely grazed Theo's egg with it. Each time the shell of Theo's egg caved in. Tiggie had won.

"She always does. She manages every year," Theo said with a wry face. "I want to know one thing, Tiggie. Is it strength or is it skill?"

There was a complacent smile on Tiggie's lips. "Both," she said. She covered his hand fleetingly with hers. "And a little luck, my dear," she added.

Theo held his vanquished egg aloft. "And next year."

"And the year after that," Tiggie said in a low voice. "And the next, and the next, until . . ." Ersi saw their eyes lock for an instant.

Theo cleared his throat and raised his glass. "As the Apostle Paul said, 'O grave, where is thy victory? O death, where is thy sting?'" He emptied his glass with a single gulp.

In the silence that followed, Ersi was aware of a sudden joy inside her, like a rocket ready to burst. It was as though the weight of the stone that covered the tomb had miraculously been lifted, the darkness dispersed. She bit her lips. Was it wrong to feel this way so soon after her mother's death?

Across the bowl of glowing, blood-coloured eggs and the trembling flame of the candles, Tiggie's eyes were fixed on her.

"I never understood it before," Ersi said slowly.

They waited for her to go on.

"I mean, what the Resurrection really means." She could hear her own voice blundering on. "Tonight it was all so close and so true, even with all the shouting and the guns going off and the fireworks."

"But how could you possibly have understood it, then?" Tiggie said.

"You mean, because it isn't the same in New York as it is here in Greece?"

"Perhaps. Although it's not really that. You had never been touched by death before."

She stared at Tiggie, feeling as though she had been jabbed by a hot wire.

"Living, dying," Tiggie went on steadily. "How can the one have any meaning unless you have been through the other? They are the two sides of the same golden coin."

"The ancients knew that," Theo put in. "How can there be a new life without a death? If the god does not die, how can he be born again? When you plant a grain of wheat in the ground, how can there be a new green blade unless the seed dies?" He broke off and refilled his glass. "But we already know all that," he said. "Don't we?"

Did we? She wondered. She was thinking of her mother.

"But it wasn't fair!" she cried. "Why did it have to be so soon?"

It was Tiggie who answered. "Whenever it happens," she said, "it always seems too soon."

Ersi sat there in silence, thinking of Ismene. She knew that Tiggie and Theo were also thinking of her. Outside, in the dark streets of the village, the last of the fireworks were still going off.

10 *Persephone*

She woke late. She had slept soundly, not like the dead this time, but like a lamb in the fold. And it was the smell of roasting lamb that was coming through the shutters.

It was Easter Sunday.

Tiggie had said that a nice leg of lamb prepared in the oven ought to do very well for the three of them. Every other household in the village, however, seemed to be roasting a whole lamb out of doors, turning it on a spit. Fires crackled in every direction. Beside each fire a radio was turned on. Music blared everywhere. From her bedroom window it seemed as though the whole village was having a party.

She went downstairs. Theo and Tiggie were already there. She wanted to go and find Lefteris. She might even take him one of their eggs. But Theo said, "As soon as you've had your breakfast, I'm taking you out. You'll want to see what's going on."

"I don't really think I need any breakfast this morning."

"Then take her with you now," Tiggie told him. "By the time you get back I'll have everything ready."

"Wouldn't you like me to stay and help you?" Ersi asked.

"Not really. And Theo is chafing to get out of the house and make his rounds."

They halted for a moment outside Kyria Dimitra's door.

It was closed. "She seems to have visitors just now," Theo said.

In front of Aghios Nikolas a vast red egg had been set up with HAPPY EASTER painted across it. From it emerged a life-sized cardboard figure of the risen Christ, one hand raised in blessing. Greek flags had been strung up everywhere. They streamed from flagpoles on the balconies. There were garlands of little paper ones strung across the narrow streets. It was as though thousands of blue-and-white flags had blossomed overnight, like morning glories.

Wherever they looked, a party was taking place under the fluttering flags. The men sat around, glasses of wine in their hands, taking turns at working the handles of the spits. There was an art to it. You had to rotate the spit, not too fast and yet not too slowly, so that the meat got roasted evenly. Meanwhile, the women bustled out of their kitchens bearing plates of food and jugs of wine. Smoke rose to the sky, bearing with it the reek of sizzling fat, while all the dogs and cats of the neighbourhood prowled around the edges of the group. They knew what was coming and they were waiting for their share. When Theo appeared with Ersi, great shouts greeted them. "Come and join us!"

Wine was poured and toasts called out even before they sat down. Plates heaped with salad and bread and cheese were passed in their direction. At one moment something was held out to her at the end of a fork. It was a chunk of lamb, crusted with crisp skin.

She recalled the bloody carcasses strung outside the butcher shops the day before, and how she and Lefteris had sworn not to touch a single morsel. "No, thank you," she said. But no one heard her. The roast lamb was popped into her mouth. It was tender and absolutely delicious.

They moved on to other groups. Sometimes it was one family, with countless cousins and in-laws. Sometimes it was several families together and you couldn't be sure who was related to whom, or even who was the host. It didn't seem to matter. Everyone had contributed something: wine, egg salad, chopped-up lettuce drenched in oil and lemon juice, or lambs' liver and lights roasted with pungent herbs and served with a dab of mustard. Considering all that Ersi was being pressed to take, it was a good thing that she hadn't eaten any breakfast. She was a little alarmed at the glasses of wine that Theo tossed down, although he didn't seem to be any the worse for it.

At last they were on their way home. How long was it since they had set out? Just then a voice called, "Great doings, eh? Now you have to come and take a glass of wine with Barba Kostas!"

He stood outside his house, an earthenware jug in his hand. His cheeks were flushed. His black eyes gleamed at them from under his bushy brows. Greek dance music poured from a cassette.

He raised his glass. He wished them "Many years, and good ones!" Half the village, as Ersi saw, seemed to have squeezed into Barba Kostas's courtyard, sitting around among his pots of flowers.

After Theo had drunk to the health of everyone present, and at Barba Kostas's insistence even Ersi had taken a sip of his wine, the cassette was turned up. The music was loud enough to tear the sky apart. Barba Kostas planted his cane in a tub of petunias and stood there perfectly motionless, waiting for the beat.

Then he whipped out a handkerchief and began to dance by himself, letting the handkerchief dangle from one hand. After a moment Savvas got up and joined him, taking hold of the other end, followed by the Nettle's son in his fine new red jacket. Soon a lot of others were also dancing, even the Inseparable Enemies, who did not speak to each other as they linked hands. Apostolos the postman leaped into the circle to join the rest.

"What about Lord John Bull?" someone shouted. So then Theo took his turn. Ersi was pulled out of her chair and was caught up in it, taking her place in the line as though it were the most natural thing in the world. Vassilis the shepherd was next to her, barefoot as always, and grinning. She followed his steps. The high, shrill music went on, and all the time Barba Kostas never flagged or missed a beat. The figures he performed became more and more intricate. He leaped and turned among the flower tubs as though there were no such thing as arthritis of the knees, as though he had never needed to use a stick in his life. It was not for nothing that his nickname in the village was The Dancer. "Who says that I have one foot in the grave and the other on a banana skin?" he shouted. "I can still dance!"

Theo and Ersi, out of breath, dropped out as did some of the others, but the dancing went on. Newcomers stepped in to take their places. At one moment a staid couple broke into the circle. They were from Athens. As they danced, their air of city importance dropped away. The woman kicked off her high-heeled shoes. Her husband wriggled out of his jacket and danced in his shirtsleeves. They were villagers again, like everyone else.

Two foreigners made their brief appearance at the end of the line. They laughed self-consciously. Ersi could tell that they thought dancing like Greeks was easy. All the same, something about their movements was not right. When they left off, the Greeks applauded them politely and offered them wine.

Demos, who had been watching from the sidelines, shook his head. "You have to be born to it," he told Ersi.

"What about me?"

"You?" he said. "You knew. You did the steps right. You have it in your blood. When you were out there you were just like one of us."

Theo said at last that it was time to get back to Tiggie. Ersi had taken only a small sip of Barba Kostas's wine, but her head was already beginning to spin. Where had Lefteris been? He always walked with lithe, cat-like steps, like a dancer's. She was sure he would have shone at Barba Kostas's.

Tiggie was waiting. The table was set. The house, like the rest of the village, was filled with the fragrance of roasted lamb. She had prepared it with garlic and rosemary and basted it with lemon juice. Ersi had been sure she could not possibly eat another mouthful, but suddenly she was hungry again.

"Before we sit down," Tiggie said, "I wish one of you would go to Kyria Dimitra." She had covered a plate with a white linen napkin. On it was a small pyramid of red eggs, decorated with flowers from the garden.

"Why couldn't we invite her to eat with us?" Ersi asked.

Tiggie shook her head. "She would never accept."

"Why not, since she is all alone?"

"Kyria Dimitra doesn't like to be beholden to anyone for anything," Tiggie answered. "This is only a token."

Ersi slipped into Dimitra's courtyard and through the open door of the house.

Kyria Dimitra, she saw, was not alone, after all.

She sat on the edge of her bed. Beside her was a young woman wearing a pale yellow blouse the colour of daffodils, a green skirt and brand new shoes of bright green. She had long dark hair and dark brimming eyes. Dimitra clasped her hands between both of her own. Tears of joy streamed down her furrowed cheeks. Ersi knew at once that it must be Dimitra's daughter.

When had she arrived in the village? Who had brought her? How long would she stay?

She quietly set Tiggie's offering on the table near the door and went away. With the stirrings of spring, Persephone had returned to her mother from the dark underside of the world.

11   *A Sleeping Giant*

"I looked for you everywhere, Lefteris, even in church. Where were you?"

"With Marigoula. I couldn't leave her by herself."

They had met out beyond the pine forest, beside the grave of the unknown cat.

"What about the books? Did you find out anything?"

"Nothing. But I have my suspicions."

"Never mind," she said quickly. "I'll bring you others."

"It's not the same thing," he told her. "Besides . . ." He broke off. "Did you tell your uncle?"

"That they disappeared? No."

Lefteris still looked worried. "Did they have his name in them?"

"I don't think so. Does it matter?"

"It's just something I thought of," he said, but he seemed relieved.

They didn't stay there long that day. Lefteris's eyes kept darting past her. She could see that he was in a hurry to go off.

"Why, Lefteris?"

"Why what?"

"Why are you so restless? Is it the books?"

He grimaced. "The books. The eyes of Panaghiotis. Everything."

Before he left she asked, "Will I see you at the party tomorrow?"

"What party?"

"I thought you would know. It's at Evvie's house. Her mother told Tiggie that all the young people of the village would be there."

"All except me," Lefteris said.

"Weren't you invited?"

"I know Evvie and her friends." His lips pressed into a disdainful line. "I wouldn't go, even if they sent me a printed invitation."

"Then I won't go, either!"

"That's silly. You have to go on account of your aunt. At least then you'll see what I mean."

Evvie was a pretty girl, dark and very animated. At one moment during the party she drew Ersi aside. "Are you having a good time?" Then, without waiting for an answer, she said, "We thought it would be nice to have you in our group. But there's that Lefteris."

"What about Lefteris?"

"Well, he's your friend, isn't he?"

"Yes. Why?"

Evvie laughed. "Well, he is such a strange boy. For one thing, he's not interested in the same things as everyone else. And then, maybe you don't know this, but his father ran away to England, where he is working against our government. My uncle, the Mayor, says our government is doing a lot of good for the village, all these new roads, and I don't know what else they promised. So he shouldn't talk that way, should he?"

"Maybe he has his reasons," Ersi said.

Evvie gave her an odd look. "Well," she said, "it's not very patriotic, is it?"

"It depends on what you mean by patriotic."

Evvie hadn't talked to her after that, only to say goodbye

when it was time for her to leave. Her mother smiled at Ersi, but Evvie didn't.

The next day, when Lefteris asked her what it had been like, she said, "Oh, it was just another party."

Festive Greek flags had burst out once more all over the village. This time, however, they seemed different. Perhaps it was because, instead of Christ rising triumphantly out of a red egg, there were posters of the Junta soldier with his bayonet. Loudspeakers hung from the trees that bordered the main square, and a wooden platform had been set up there, festooned with banners that read GREECE FOR CHRISTIAN GREEKS!

Down on the quay was a freshly painted sign proclaiming its new name.

"*The Avenue of the Twenty-first of April.* That's today. What's going to happen, Lefteris?"

"The usual goings-on," he said. "The Naval Cadets' Band will play military music. All the village notables will be sitting on the platform to demonstrate their loyalty to the regime."

"Like who?"

"More than you might think. First of all there will be the Mayor and his whole family."

"Including Evvie, I suppose. I'd like to show her what *patriotic* really means."

"Then," he went on, "there will be our political representative back for the day from Athens; and the police, of course. And the Horse Fly."

"Who?"

"You know, that's what I call Panaghiotis. And the schoolteachers. And the Harbourmaster. And the priests, to bless the ceremony."

"Even the *pappas* from Aghios Ioannis?"

"No, not him. He's all right. And they'll have all the schoolchildren marching in the parade. The politician from

Athens last year spoke for two hours," he added. "I timed him."

Ersi surveyed the bandstand and made a face. "I wish we could do something! We couldn't stop it, I know, but at least if we could only jam the works a little, and slow it down!"

"Like what?"

"Like tearing down those awful posters."

"There are too many."

They had edged up to the speakers' platform. "Maybe we could disconnect the loudspeakers. How about those wires? Pull one, Lefteris."

"I don't know which one to pull."

"Then *what*? We have to do something!"

Every time they moved closer to the platform one of the policemen appeared to warn them away. But just before they left the square Ersi whispered, "Quick! Give me your black crayon."

"What are you going to do with it?"

"Just hand it to me. No one's watching just now."

She reached out and scrawled a big, lop-sided swastika over one of the posters. Then she walked as casually as she could out of the square, leaving Lefteris to follow her, wide-eyed. When he caught up with her, he asked, "What was that for?"

"Don't you know? The swastika was the symbol of Nazi fascism. My mother used to say that the Colonels are nothing more than a cheap copy of Hitler."

When she returned home Theo muttered that the celebration should have taken place the day before.

"Why?"

"It would have been more appropriate. April the twentieth is Hitler's birthday."

There was a warning look from Tiggie. "Theo! Your blood pressure!"

Ersi decided that it was not the time to tell him about

her swastika.

He subsided reluctantly. "Is everything ready?" he asked.

"I think so," Tiggie said. "I packed the picnic basket with some sandwiches, fruit, a thermos of coffee, and the last of the Easter eggs."

Ersi stared at them. Were they going to the square to watch the ceremony?

"Do we have to go?" she asked.

"*We*," Theo said, "are going on a little fishing trip." He handed Ersi the basket. He took charge of the fishing lines, the plastic bucket with the bait, and a coil of rope for the boat. "Take sweaters along, both of you. The weather might change." Then he handed Ersi a canvas bag. "I nearly forgot this," he said.

"What's in it?"

"Just some books, three or four."

"Three or four heavy books, just for a little fishing trip?"

He was intercepted by a look from Tiggie. "Let's get started, while it's still early," he said, "before we're noticed."

There was not much activity at that hour along the Avenue of the Twenty-first of April. A couple of children in their school uniforms, wearing white gloves and white knee socks and carrying flags, scurried in the other direction to take their places before the celebration started. Everyone else, it seemed, was already in the square. She could picture Lefteris among them, scowling.

Theo's boat was tied up at the quay. Its name, *Antigone*, was painted on its stern. It was a French craft, a Zodiac, only four metres in length. Theo said it was a very satisfactory size for them. The best thing about the Zodiac was that it was made of rubber. "You blow it up in the spring," he said, "and when winter comes you let the air out and store it." He settled them in the boat and started the engine. After a few coughs it began to chug out of the harbour.

From the water, the village looked unfamiliar, not at all the way it appeared from the saddle of Pegasus. It was like some other, smaller, place. The air was so clear they could hear the Naval Cadets' Band tuning up. Someone was testing the loudspeakers in the square. Otherwise, quiet pressed over everything like a dome of glass. Only one fishing boat was out that morning, but it was too far off for them to hear its motor or to see whose it might be. The shore was deserted, except for the solitary figure of a man making his way beside the water, his thin trousers flapping against his legs.

The little boat shot forward. The village vanished. On one side lay the open gulf, the mountain rising behind it. On their right was only a string of small, rocky bays, stretching back as far as the pine forest. Gulls flapped around them, mewing like cats.

Theo shaded his eyes and looked around. Then he tossed the anchor overboard and got out the fishing gear and the bait. When he offered Ersi a line, she shook her head. "If I catch anything, I can't bear to take it off the hook," she said.

"That's exactly how I feel," Tiggie remarked, lighting a cigarette and settling back against a cushion, the brim of her straw hat shading her eyes. Theo busied himself with his lines. Neither of them seemed interested in the bag with the books. Ersi was content to be sitting there in the quiet morning, the Zodiac rocking gently under her while she stared at the coastline. She had always considered scenery boring. But the rocky Greek landscape was more than mere scenery. Figures loomed out of it under the constantly shifting light.

The hills opposite them had a peculiar conformation, like a human shape stretched out on its back against the sky. Hawks hovered and skimmed high above it.

Through the puff of smoke from his pipe Theo said, "The villagers call it *The Sleeping Giant.*"

She stared at the Sleeping Giant. "Someone," and she meant Lefteris, "told me that the Colonels, at the very beginning, said that for the time being Greece was like a patient after a serious operation; that it would have to remain in a plaster cast until it recovered."

"Seven years have passed," Theo said. "The plaster cast hasn't been removed."

"In all that time couldn't anybody do anything?"

"How can you fight back when someone is holding a revolver to your head and you're in a plaster cast?"

"You could have left. My mother said all the time that she didn't know why you stayed. She kept hoping you would come to us, to America."

Theo looked thoughtful. "We had our passports ready. Lots of our friends had already left. But so far, the police haven't bothered us. We are too old, it would seem, or too private. Or else they have never come across your aunt's file."

She stared at Tiggie, who continued to puff her cigarette.

"Didn't you know? She has a police record. She was in the resistance movement against the Germans during the Second World War."

"What's wrong with that?" Ersi asked.

"The Colonels strongly disapprove. Some of the resistance was formed by the Left. Not all, however. A lot of us were involved simply because we hated the Nazis and wanted our country free of them."

"No matter what happens now," Tiggie put in, "I refuse to leave. I'm too old for exile. The Germans didn't succeed in killing me and I don't see why those Greek fascists should drive me out. I was born a Greek. I might as well die a Greek."

It was exactly, Ersi thought, what Ismene used to say.

"Personally," Theo said, "I find it possible to ignore the Colonels. All governments, good or bad, are there to be ignored. It's the only way to survive."

"What about those who don't survive?" Tiggie flung out. "Like those students at the Polytechnical School in Athens last November who broadcast anti-Junta slogans from the model radio station they built? The Army sent out tanks. They crashed through the iron gates of the campus. To this day nobody knows how many of those students were killed."

"All the same," Theo said, "survival is an internal affair, a matter of personal philosophy."

Tiggie tossed her cigarette into the water. She lit another one. "Just listen to him! He's saying survival has nothing to do with government!"

Theo turned to Ersi. "Your great-aunt Antigone," he told her, "is like the ancient lady after whom she was named. She is all for political involvement. Being a true Greek, she maintains that everything is political. She is still paying for it."

"I would do it again," Tiggie maintained, "if I had to."

"Why do you think she walks with a limp?" Theo pursued. "During the German occupation she had a mimeograph machine hidden in her Athens basement. She printed handbills on it with news of the resistance movement. She was passing them out on a street corner when a German bullet stopped her."

"I didn't know that!" Ersi exclaimed. She had never thought to ask about Tiggie's lameness.

"It didn't stop me for long," Tiggie said. "Anyway, I couldn't do anything else because I had Ismene to look after. And what about you, Theo? Didn't you try to escape to Egypt to join the Greek forces in the Middle East?"

"I wanted to fight for freedom, not for politics."

"It's the same thing," Tiggie said.

Ersi decided that she was like Tiggie. She would have to act, to take a stand, to do something, even if it was only passing out handbills at street corners! Oh, if only she had managed to put the loudspeakers out of commission, instead of just scrawling that silly swastika!

From the village they could hear the speakers blaring in the square. The boat rocked gently in the water. Tiggie scanned the coast. She said, "I think it's time, Theo."

He drew in his fishing lines. "Not a bite! All the smart Greek fish have swum off to some other sea." He hauled in the anchor and started the engine. The boat shot back in the direction of the pine forest.

The celebration in the square was still going on. So why were they going back? Hadn't the whole point of the fishing trip been to avoid it?

They were halfway there, opposite the deepest of the rocky coves, when once again she caught sight of the man who had been trudging along the shore. Now he sat by the side of the water, holding a fishing line. As the boat veered towards him, she saw that it was Solon.

"Why didn't you stop before?" she asked Theo.

"It wasn't the right moment. You never know who might be watching."

Theo was exaggerating, just like Lefteris. Out here, in this quiet, deserted spot, who could have noticed them?

Solon greeted them with a cautious wave.

"It is better to speak in English," Theo said quickly. "These days even the crabs have ears."

Solon asked in a low voice, "How is the fishing?"

"I brought you some nice fat ones."

But there hadn't been a solitary bite, Ersi thought.

"I couldn't bring more," Theo said. "It would be too conspicuous."

Tiggie produced the bag with the books. Solon clutched it in both hands. His worn face lit up, just as Lefteris's had when she mentioned the books she had brought for him. "I was able to pick up a few volumes here and there in the village," Solon said. "I have gone through all of them a hundred times. You didn't forget the Aristotle? I can't trust my memory any more and there are some passages I want to read again."

"I brought you a nice clean edition."

Solon glanced cautiously around. "The parade will be over soon. The police don't like to keep me out of their sight."

Theo nodded. "I was careful not to let anyone suspect that we know each other," he said. "Anyway, I was glad to get your message."

Solon gave him a wry grin. "I wasn't sure that you would find the cigarette packet when I tossed it into your boat."

"As a matter of fact," Tiggie put in, "he nearly threw it away without looking at it."

"Has anything new happened?" Theo asked. "Are they treating you all right?"

"They don't bother me, really. The only thing is that I don't get any news of my wife. I worry about her. She's not well." He loaded the books into his shoulder bag. Then he raised his hand in a quick gesture of farewell. He turned and trudged off in his worn-out canvas shoes, his threadbare trousers flapping against his ankles.

The sea around them was a flat dead calm, but it was suddenly chilly there in the Zodiac. Ersi was glad that Tiggie had brought her pullover. She tied it around her shoulders.

"Do you think it will last forever?" she asked. "I mean, will he ever be able to go home to his wife?"

"It will have to end," Tiggie said. "The Colonels and their like come and go. We stay on."

Someone had said something like that to her before, but Ersi could not remember now who it had been.

"But who are *we*?" she asked. "Against *them*?"

"Theo. And you. And I." Tiggie regarded her steadily. "And there are others, more than you might possibly think, all waiting to see them go."

And Lefteris, Ersi was thinking. But they were all just waiting. No one was doing anything about it. They would have to stop talking, and act. Maybe Lefteris could think of something they could do.

Tiggie reached for the picnic basket.

After eating, they threw the crumbs into the sea.

"Look!" cried Theo. "Here they come now!"

As from nowhere, hundreds of little fish appeared, flashing through the water to engulf the crumbs of bread. The sea was alive with them.

The hullabaloo in the village had died down. It was time to go back. As the Zodiac pulled away from the cove, Ersi turned her gaze for the last time towards the coast where the giant lay spread out, sleeping against the sky.

12 *After the Parade*

She was in the square with Lefteris the next day, watching the banners and the flags being taken down.

She had brought him more books, but he had accepted them indifferently, not saying anything. It was as though learning English didn't matter to him any more. He hadn't even bothered to stick a flower in his shirt pocket.

The platform was dismantled, along with the loud-speakers. They watched the members of the Naval Cadets' Band go off in the military transport which had brought them, and the dignitaries from Athens being chauffeured back to the city in a large black Mercedes with official number plates.

"Well, what was it like?"

"The worst of it was the slogans we had to shout. 'Our superb warrior race will never die!' 'Let the flowers of regeneration bloom out of the debris of the old regime of falsehood!' 'Democracy, without the pollution of foreign ideologies and propaganda!' 'Unity, work, peace, progress!' They would never recognise real progress if you hit them on their heads with it. They think it just means more cement." He snorted. "Do you have to shout such things in America?"

"No."

"What's more, none of the other children wanted me to

108

march with them. One of them spat on the ground at my feet. He said, 'I don't want people to see me next to the son of traitors.'"

"Who was that? Evvie?"

"She was up front, carrying the flag. It was a friend of hers."

"So what did you answer?"

"I told him to shove off before I gave him one. Only," he added, blushing, "that wasn't exactly the word I used."

She couldn't help laughing. Then she said in a serious voice, "You should have been in Alabama during the struggle for civil rights."

"Alabama? What's that?"

"It's a state in the South. People went there from every part of the country to march and to demonstrate for the black people. Until then they weren't treated like everybody else. They still aren't."

"Why not?"

"Only on account of being black. The children even had to go to separate schools."

"In America? I can't believe such a thing."

"It's true. Everything in America isn't perfect."

"And? What happened then?"

"After that things began to change. But it wasn't easy. Churches were bombed, with children in them. They killed a black leader, a minister who believed in nonviolence. Some of the marchers were murdered by gangs of racists while the police just looked on and didn't stop it."

"Were you there?"

"I was too young. But my father went."

There was an eager gleam in his eyes. "What was it like?"

"He tells in one of his stories how he heard a little black girl call out to her friend, 'Hurry up, Emmeline, or we'll be too late to get arrested with the rest of our class!'"

He stared at her. "They arrested a whole class? What about that little girl? Wasn't she afraid?"

"Maybe she was, but she was fighting for justice and freedom. I think she must have been proud."

He thought about it for a moment. Then he said, "I would be, too." He added, "At least people were able to go and help the struggle by marching along with them. I wish I could know your father. I think he must be a little bit like mine."

Now that the Twenty-first of April was over, the village looked just the way it always had. The new sign on the quay, however, was still there. "That means the new name is official," Lefteris pointed out. When they passed the coffee house, the Argonauts were all there, rattling the dice on their backgammon boards. "You see?" he said. "They look as though nothing unusual had happened."

"All the same," she said, "there must have been some in the village, like us, who weren't in the square yesterday. Some of them must have refused to shout 'Long live the Colonels!'"

"Maybe." Lefteris shrugged. "But who would know? The square was packed."

"I think there ought to be a secret signal," she said, "so that you could tell who was on our side." Suddenly she cried out, "Look! That table at the far end!"

"What about it? I don't see anything. It's empty."

"That's what I mean. It's where Solon always sits."

When Ersi turned to go home, Lefteris said, "Marigoula is waiting to see you. I told her I would bring you back with me."

Marigoula lived at the end of a narrow lane, facing the Widows' Bay. The Widows' Bay was a deep inlet. According to Lefteris it was called that because in the old days, when the sailing ships returned from their long voyages, the widows of the village gathered there to wait, so that their mourning garments would not cast a pall over the joyous reunions on the quay.

It was a small house. Everything was freshly white-washed, even the cobblestones outside. On their way they passed Rinió and Katya, each sitting alone outside her own house. They stared at her.

Marigoula was small and round, and her round eyes were like currants embedded in her face. She was wearing black, but she had pinned a brooch with a coloured stone to her shawl for the occasion. A smile broke across her face when she caught sight of them.

"So you are Lefteris's friend! Come closer, my child, so that I can see you properly. My old eyes are not what they used to be."

Ersi stepped closer, Marigoula reached out and patted her cheek.

"Lefteris tells me that you are Kyria Antigone's niece. I never saw your mother, but I did know your uncle Theo when he was a boy. I was young, too, then. That was before I went to Athens to work in Lefteris's grand-mother's house. I used to follow him with my eyes all the time. Of course I didn't think he even knew I existed. He used to walk around the village when he came as though the whole place belonged to him, like a young god, always talking to different people, forever asking questions. The village was different, then." She smiled, remembering. "It was a little world all unto itself."

Lefteris stood nearby. He shifted his weight from one foot to the other, looking proud and embarrassed at the same time.

They went inside the house. In the front room stood a big brass bed, where Lefteris slept. "After all," Marigoula said, "he is the man of the house." Ersi could see a suitcase under it. It would be the suitcase his mother had packed for him to take to England. On the wall hung a heavy frame with an enlarged photograph: Vangelis.

Marigoula motioned to the two of them to sit on the bed.

"Let me tell you about Lefteris," she said, lowering herself onto a straight wooden chair. "He is a boy made of pure gold. But he is also a little donkey."

Lefteris leaped up. "Oh, Marigoula! Not now."

"Sit down and be quiet." She turned back to Ersi. "These are bad times for all of us," she went on, "but it is not the first time I know. I have lived through other bad times. It is not easy for the boy, waiting here and living in the house of an old woman."

He started to protest again, but she silenced him with a flap of her hand. "And now that he is getting so big, there is not much more that I can do for him. That is why I am happy that he has found a friend in the village at last. It is not right for a boy to be so bitter and alone. Yesterday, in the parade, he was like a porcupine, with all his spikes sticking out. He even got into a fight with one of the other boys."

"I didn't fight with him. I just told him off."

"I saw you both. It was as good as a fight."

Ersi said, "He didn't tell me that you went to the celebration, Kyria Marigoula."

"I had to go, for the boy's sake. All the others had someone there to watch them and be proud."

"I begged her not to go," Lefteris put in heatedly. "What's there to be proud of, hearing us shout all those stupid slogans?"

Marigoula sighed. "I only went to see him and the other children."

"Nevertheless . . . " Lefteris began.

"There is no 'nevertheless'," Marigoula said.

"But somebody has to do something!" Ersi cried.

"Like what?" Marigoula asked. "Like those poor students with their model radio station? In the end they were killed. What could they do against the tear gas and the tanks?"

"Nevertheless," Lefteris said once more, "it's time we

showed them."

"What are you talking about? Supposing you are a little hero and get arrested. What will that prove? Isn't it enough that your father and your mother and your sister cannot come back to the country where they belong? Isn't it enough that after so long you cannot go and join them where they are?"

"Well," said Lefteris, "I'm tired of waiting."

"Do as you like, then." She glanced up at the photograph and crossed herself. "My poor Vangelis, may God forgive him for his sins, if he hadn't wanted to be a hero he would have been alive all these years." She wiped her eyes on a corner of her shawl. "Perhaps I have never learned to read or write, but in my lifetime I have learned to sharpen my soul on the whetstone of patience."

Lefteris walked Ersi halfway home. "Patience!" he echoed scornfully. "I am worn out with the whetstone of patience. If only there was something we could do, something to show them that we aren't all paralysed in their plaster cast!"

"I know where we can start," she said.

He kicked listlessly at a stone. "Where? With what?"

"With that sign on the quay. I can't stand the sight of it."

"Neither can I!"

"Well?"

They looked at each other.

"When?"

"Tonight. Why wait?"

He fixed her with an intent, narrow look. "Do you mean it?"

"Of course I mean it."

"Even if it means being arrested like those black children in what was that place?"

"Alabama," she said. "Listen. I'll meet you on the quay just after midnight. It ought to be deserted by then."

"How can you get out of the house without your aunt and uncle knowing?"

"They'll be in bed. I could manage to slip out long enough."

"Then I'll see you there? Tonight? You're sure?"

"Yes. Wait for me if I'm late."

He hesitated.

"Are you really certain you want to do it? We'll be sticking our necks out."

"Isn't that what they're for?" she said.

She was worried all day, but she tried not to show it. At one moment Tiggie asked, "Is anything wrong?"

"Wrong?"

Tiggie left it at that.

She was careful to leave the garden door slightly open so that it wouldn't creak when she went out, and she went to bed with her clothes on. In bed she glanced at her wristwatch every five minutes. How the hands crawled!

Then it was time.

When she reached the quay, Lefteris was already there. He had brought a screwdriver with him. They listened for footsteps, not daring to speak to each other. But no one else was out at that hour on the Avenue of the Twenty-first of April.

She whispered, "How are we going to do it?"

"I'll have to stand on your shoulders."

She tried not to let her knees buckle while he pried the sign off the wall. Please, don't let anyone come now, she thought. Then he had jumped down and was holding it out to her.

"Maybe you want to keep it," he whispered, "for a souvenir."

"It's not really the kind of souvenir I want for my collection."

He sent it sailing off beyond the edge of the quay. They

watched it curve through the air, between the masts of the fishing boats, before it struck the water and sank. Then, without a word, they started to run in opposite directions.

It was all over. They had done it, and it had been so simple. She was positive that no one had seen them. All the same, as she slid through the shadows of the garden, she wondered how it was possible that the entire sleeping village had not been awakened by the thunderous pounding of her heart.

13   *At the Lonely House*

In the morning she went down to the quay. There was the empty place where the sign had been, but no one seemed to be paying any attention to it. Didn't they realise what had happened? Or did they all assume that its being taken down had been a routine part of the end of the celebration? She didn't see Lefteris anywhere.

It turned windy that afternoon. She set out on Pegasus. But Lefteris didn't show up at their meeting place, so she found herself pedalling alone in the direction of the Lonely House.

When she left behind her the last houses that straggled up the rocky hill, there was no other sign of life, not even a tethered donkey. There were only rusted pots, plastic bags flapping from the dry thistles on which they had been caught, smashed bottles, a battered baby carriage.

The last few yards were so rough that she had to get down and wheel Pegasus along. When she finally reached the Lonely House she saw that it was wide open to the weather. The door banged back and forth. The only remaining shutter creaked in the wind.

She peered through the doorway. No one was there. As she crossed the threshold, her breathing quickened. There was definitely something spooky about the place.

Cautiously, she stared around. It was only one room. In

a corner stood a toilet without a lid, a plastic bucket next to it. There was a metal cot with an old army blanket. The thin mattress had been slashed. Its wadded cotton guts littered the floor. In the middle of the room was a stained formica table with an oil lamp and a cup of coffee on it. The coffee was cold. There was a single chair with a plywood seat and shelves made out of old vegetable crates. Books were strewn across the floor. Against the far wall a door with blistered paint had been stretched across two saw-horses. It had a small primus stove with an enamel sauce-pan sitting on it, a few chipped plates, a washbowl, and a few grocery supplies. There was no electricity, no sink. A tap had been cemented into the window sill. It dripped. From a nail above it hung a towel.

Someone had taken pains to keep everything neat and clean. And yet, who could possibly have lived in such desolation? And why was the mattress slashed, and the books strewn about?

Cluck! A scrawny chicken stalked across the cement floor. Ersi jumped. She waved her arm. The chicken squawked and fluttered out through the window. Then she caught sight of the book lying in the corner, near the door.

It lay open, its cover splattered with white-ringed chicken droppings. Gingerly, she picked it up. It was printed in ancient Greek on the left-hand side and in English on the opposite page. She turned to the title: *The Politics of Aristotle.* A name just below it had been scratched out. Theo's.

So the Lonely House was the house of Solon's exile.

But where was Solon?

She brushed most of the chicken droppings from the book cover with a crumpled Kleenex from her pocket and sat down on the door sill to wait for him. The book flopped open. Some of the passages had been scored in the margin with a pencil.

Tiggie always said that when Theo read a book he

handled it as carefully as if he intended to return it to the bookstore for credit. It must have been Solon who had marked it. Some lines leaped out at her from the page, not only marked but underscored.

"Tyrants maintain their authority over their subjects by making them incapable of action. Nobody will attempt the overthrow of tyranny when all are incapable of action . . ."

A dog barked outside somewhere. Then she heard a stealthy footstep. Someone was watching her.

She looked up into a sallow face that could have used a shave. One of the eyes had a slight squint.

Lefteris's Horse Fly, Panaghiotis!

He said at last, "You're Lord John Bull's niece, aren't you?"

She nodded.

"So. And what are you doing here?"

She got to her feet. "Nothing. The door was open."

His expression was sly and knowing. "You came to see him, didn't you?"

"Came to see whom?"

He was beside her now, standing over her. "You can skip the cleverness. I know what you're up to."

"I don't know what you're talking about. I'm not 'up to' anything."

He fixed her with his squinting eye. "You're not fooling me, my girl. You've come to bring more books, most likely with messages in them." He let out an abrasive laugh. "Well, you won't be able to deliver them this time. He's gone."

Her heart bounded. Had Solon managed to escape, to get off to his friends in Italy? She kept her face frozen and expressionless. "Who's gone?"

"Your friend the judge. Didn't you know? They took him away this morning."

She was not going to give Panaghiotis the satisfaction of asking him who had taken Solon, and where. She fixed an innocuous smile on her face. "I didn't bring anyone anything. I didn't even know that someone lived here."

He shot her a glance of disbelief. "What's that book you're holding?"

"I found it here. Someone must have left it."

He grabbed it from her. "I didn't see it when we came for him," he muttered to himself. He shook it, like a terrier shaking a rat that was not quite dead. Nothing fell out. Then he pawed roughly through it, poring over the marked passages. "What does that say?" he demanded, shoving it into her face. "It's foreign."

"You can see for yourself. It's in Greek on the other side."

"Greek?" He scowled at the page. "I can't make it out."

"It's ancient Greek."

He peered at the text. It was clear that ancient Greek was indecipherable to him. It could have just as well been Japanese, or Russian. "I can see one thing. It's about politics. It's probably Communist propaganda like those other books we found." He slapped the book shut and shoved it under his armpit.

"It's not Communist propaganda. It's Aristotle."

"You don't say! And what is this Aristotle's other name? Is he a friend of Lord John Bull's?" He dug his fingers into her arm. "All right," he said. "You're coming with me."

"Where?"

"To the police station. We'll find out what kind of Greek is in that book. The Chief will want to ask you a few questions as well!"

She planted her feet and looked into his squinty little eyes. "What questions?"

"You'll find out when we get there. He already knows about those books you left in the bushes, and about the Twenty-first of April when your uncle and aunt met the judge beyond the pine forest."

"Oh, that! We went fishing. We were in the Zodiac. He was there on the shore. He was fishing also."

"No more of your smart answers! What did they talk about?"

"They talked about fishing."

"Fishing?"

"Yes. About catching fish."

His eyes bored into hers. "About certain very big fish, eh?"

"I don't know what you mean. Anyway, there weren't any fish that day."

"You know very well what I'm talking about. They talked Greek, did they?"

"No. In English."

"Aha! But I knew that." He looked slyer than ever. "I am glad you have decided not to tell me any more lies. Why did they have to talk in English?"

"They just did."

His fingers dug deeper into her arm. "They didn't mention the government?"

She shook her head, wincing.

Abruptly, Panaghiotis relaxed his grip. His voice turned soft and cajoling. "Look. I can tell you're a good kid. You have brains. You grew up in America, but your mother was Greek. She must have loved Greece. Don't you love Greece, like her? You see, I know all about you. And now I simply want one little thing from you. Just tell me what they talk about."

"Who?"

"Your mother's aunt and her husband."

"When?"

"When they are alone, at home. Tell me the names of the people they talk about, the ones who are against the government, like their friend Aristotle in Athens. Just tell me that, and I'll let you go home. After that you can forget all about it and Greece will always be grateful to you."

"But they don't talk about such things," she insisted. "I don't know any names."

He regarded her with reproach. "Aren't you ashamed, my girl, protecting Communists and helping the enemies of the Greek nation?"

"What enemies? You mean Tiggie and Theo and Solon?"

"And there's your little friend Lefteris. You've been seeing him, also."

"I want you to know something," she shouted at him. "They are not Communists and they are not the enemies of Greece. They are people who believe in freedom. They are the true Greeks!"

His face clouded. "Stop shouting!" he shouted. He gripped her arm. "So you won't talk to me. But the Chief will loosen that tongue of yours at the police station. There are other things he wants to ask you about."

So they knew about the sign on the quay as well. And she was going to be arrested. She was glad. She would be doing something for justice and freedom. Lefteris would be proud of her. Her father would be proud of her also. And now she would know what it felt like to be a hero, like those Civil Rights marchers in the South.

Panaghiotis's iron fingers tightened on her arm.

Suddenly she yanked herself free. "I'm not going anywhere with you!" She kicked out at his shins and made a dash for Pegasus.

She began to pedal away furiously. "Why, the little bitch!" she heard him call after her. The bicycle hurtled along the path. Then the front wheel struck something. Pegasus crashed to the ground, sending her sprawling among the rocks and the rubbish.

Had she seen a holster bulging under Panaghiotis's windbreaker? She expected to hear the crack of a pistol any minute.

Blindly, she scrambled to her feet. She righted the

bicycle, jumped onto it and raced away against the pressure of the wind. The air snapped behind her. She turned once and looked back. Panaghiotis stood on the doorstep of the Lonely House. He loomed against the sky, his face twisted grimly.

Lefteris, she knew, wouldn't have been afraid.

They were sitting in the garden, reading. Theo caught sight of her first. "What on earth!" he exclaimed.

Tiggie said, "Get the mercurochrome and some cotton-wool from upstairs," and pushed Ersi into the kitchen. "I'll have to wash off that blood. It's streaming from your leg."

By the time Theo came stamping downstairs with half the contents of the medicine cabinet, Tiggie was able to reassure him. "She'll survive. By the time she's married she'll have forgotten all about it."

"What happened to you? Look at your hands!"

She looked up at him from the chair where Tiggie was administering to her wounds. "I met Panaghiotis," she said.

"Did he do that to you?"

"No. He only asked me about Solon."

"What did you tell him?"

"Nothing. But Panaghiotis already knows about the fishing trip, and that we spoke to him in English."

"I never caught sight of a living soul out there that day!" Tiggie said.

"Anyway," Ersi told them, "Solon is gone. They took him away this morning. Then Panaghiotis tried to find out from me what the two of you talk about at home."

"Panaghiotis," Theo fumed, "is an animal and a half!"

Tiggie warned him not to get worked up. "Remember your blood pressure."

"At least now she has seen for herself what they are really like. Nice work, isn't it, getting children to spy on their families!"

"He also found the Aristotle. He said it was Communist

propaganda. He wanted to take me to the police station, only I wouldn't go with him."

"Did he try to force you?"

"I managed to get away on Pegasus, but I fell off. And that's how I cut myself."

Tiggie and Theo looked at each other. Then, without another word, Theo got his hat and went off.

"Well?" Tiggie asked when he returned.

He hung up his hat. "Ersi will go to the police station," he announced, "but only if it is absolutely necessary, and then not without me." He also said that Solon was suspected of being the person who had taken down the sign on the quay.

Ersi felt cold. "But he didn't!" she cried.

"You don't have to tell me that," Theo said. "However, the Chief of Police informed me that Solon is now on his way to a barren island in the middle of the Aegean Sea where the sun and the jellyfish will be his only friends."

Poor Solon! Ersi thought. Had she and Lefteris been responsible for his having been taken away?

"What about the books?" Tiggie asked.

They had found two of Theo's books in the Lonely House and had confiscated them. They were in English, which no one in the police station could read. Theo managed to convince them that one of them was a detective story. The other was by a Russian author, but it was a novel that had been written long before the Russian Revolution. "They had to take my word for it," Theo said.

"They were probably hoping to find arms and explosives," Tiggie said, "and all they found was books."

"Books can be explosive enough," said Theo.

"What about the Aristotle?"

"I did my best to convince them that Aristotle was not a dangerous radical, nor was he a personal acquaintance of mine, but one of the fathers of modern philosophy, and

that the book they were holding had been written some-
time between 336 and 332. Before Christ."

Theo went on, but Ersi couldn't listen any more. She
had been waiting for him to say something about the sign
that was missing from the quay, but he never mentioned it
again.

That day Tiggie had made stuffed tomatoes and
peppers. They were just as Ismene used to make them,
without meat, and filled with rice and pine nuts and
raisins. As she ate, Ersi wondered what Solon would be
having for supper on his barren island, surrounded by
jellyfish.

14 *The Divine Fire*

"They think it was Solon who took the sign," she told Lefteris the day after it happened.

"Solon? How could they possibly have thought that? He's the last person to do such a thing."

She went on to tell him what had occurred at the Lonely House.

"You should have asked me about that place. I would have warned you," he said. "Now the Horse Fly will have that squinty eye of his on you also."

That very morning Panaghiotis had stopped him on the street. "What is this sudden thing about foreign books around here? Maybe you can explain it, since you also have a mania for reading them." So now they knew for sure what had happened to the books Ersi had left for Lefteris.

In the weeks that followed, however, Panaghiotis just looked the other way whenever he passed her in the village. Several times she and Lefteris saw him sitting with the Chief of Police outside the *kaffenion* on the square. He whispered something in the Chief's ear as they passed. She was sure he was whispering about them. Another time she ran into him near Bread and Salt's *taverna*. "Are you still around?" he called out and went swaggering off on his pointy shoes along what had been the Avenue of the Twenty-first of April.

After that she paid no attention to him. She wasn't afraid of him any more.

Lefteris said that the Horse Fly wasn't paying much attention to him either, these days. He seemed to have his mind on other things.

One day when she went to get Theo's newspaper, there was a long line ahead of her. By the time it was her turn there were no papers left. "Let's go around to the Argonauts' coffee house and see if I can take a look at somebody else's," Theo said.

Demos was there, in his baseball cap. He had been among the first in the line. He sat outside, reading the front page while his coffee got cold.

"What's the news today?" Theo asked.

"Not so good. Here, have a look for yourself."

Theo grabbed the paper and read intently for a few minutes.

"What do you think will happen now?" Demos asked him.

"Who can tell? It's a touchy business, the situation in Cyprus."

Ersi learned, as she listened, that Cyprus was a large island near the southern shore of Turkey. It had been independent, under British protection. Lately there had been flare-ups between the Greeks and the Turks who lived there. Now Greece was demanding that Cyprus should be united with Greece. "The Greek Cypriots are our blood brothers!" the Athens headlines screamed.

"How does it look to you?" Demos persisted.

Theo looked thoughtful. "I don't like all this violence. The Greeks and the Turks have lived there peacefully for so long, happy to have British passports. Now they're at each others' throats."

"Did you read where it says that Cyprus is a powder keg, that it might explode any minute?"

Theo nodded. "And who can be sure what's really

behind it, who's stirring them up? Here, take back your paper. I've read enough."

"If Cyprus does explode," Ersi asked him when they were on their way home, "what will happen then? Will it be bad for Greece?"

"It will be a bad thing for everyone concerned: Greece, Turkey, Britain, Cyprus. There is a long history of struggles between the Greeks and the Turks. But at the moment, we have enough trouble in this country as it is. I tell you one thing. If Cyprus explodes, Greece could go to war with Turkey, which would be a national disaster."

Soon posters about Cyprus were plastered all over the village. Meanwhile, the tourists began to show up, like the first early swallows announcing the coming of summer. Her father wrote every week. He said in each of his letters that he missed her, that the apartment wasn't the same without her. Honor's letters were all about school. "We're doing the Russian Revolution in History. It's even harder than when we had the French one."

On one of those early summer mornings they had an unexpected visitor.

All three of them were in the garden. Tiggie and Theo had been fussing over the amaryllis. The buds were visibly larger, but as yet they showed no signs of blooming. Tiggie happened to glance up. A tall figure stood framed in the green doorway.

"Anghelos!" she cried.

It was Anghelos Eliou, the poet from Delphi.

Ersi had never seen a poet before, but he looked the way she had always imagined a poet would. He had a radiant face and piercing amber eyes.

"Really, Anghelos," Tiggie said. "You should have let us know you were coming."

"There was no time to get a message to you," he said. "And I was suddenly possessed by a need to come down from the mountain to see the exact look of the sun as it embraces the sea." He came sailing through the doorway, followed by a thin, rather severe-looking woman who never took her eyes off him.

"Is she his wife?" Ersi asked Theo in a whisper.

"You might say so," he said. "For the time being."

When the greetings were over, Anghelos turned and saw Ersi. "And who is the girl?"

"This is Ersi, Anghelos," Tiggie said, "my grand-niece from America."

"She has a different look to her, not quite like a Greek. And yet, I should have known at once that she is Ismene's daughter." Only when he came and stood beside her did she realise that he was actually a rather short man. He fixed her with his penetrating eyes. "Do you want to be a poet?" he asked. He smiled. "I remember that your mother did, when she was your age. She would read her poems to me. She had a beautiful low voice."

Although there was no chill in the air she felt a small shiver go through her. This was something about her mother that she had never known. It was as though, for a moment, she had found her again.

"A poet? I'm not sure. I like to write, though."

His gaze remained pinned on her. "Why?"

"I don't know. Maybe it's because I like words."

He was still smiling. "When young people tell me that they want to be poets because they have something to say to the world, I always think, 'Well, perhaps . . .' But when they answer that it is because they have a passion for words, I know there is hope for them. In the beginning is always the Word. Shall I tell you an important secret which most people do not know?" He drew her towards him and lowered his voice so that the others could not overhear. "Now you will have to grow up and listen to the unspoken word as well as the spoken." He let go of her hand. "Theo!" he called out. "Where is the wine?"

"If I had known you were coming," Tiggie said, "I would have fixed lunch."

"In that case," Anghelos replied, "it is just as well that I didn't get a message to you. Now we can go out to the quay and eat at the *taverna* of Bread and Salt."

He insisted that they sit outside. Petros shoved two tables together and found chairs for them. He kept a respectful silence. It was clear from his expression that he knew who Anghelos was.

Anghelos lowered himself into the chair at the head of the table. He turned to Petros. "Which are you, Bread or Salt?"

"I am Salt, Mr Anghelos."

"Where is Bread? Tell him that an old friend wishes to speak to him."

Petros ran to get Andreas, who came blinking out into the sunshine, slightly stooped, a reserved smile on his lined face. He wiped his hands on his grease-stained apron before he shook Anghelos's hand.

"How is your frying pan?" Anghelos asked. "I remember the one you started out with, forty years ago."

"I still use the same one, Mr Anghelos. It is as good as ever. The secret is never to wash it. I give it a good wipe each time with newspaper. Water and soap are the kiss of death to a good frying pan."

Anghelos threw back his head and laughed. "And what are you going to produce for us out of it today?"

"Does anyone ask you what you are going to write today? You keep to your pen and leave me to my frying pan." He cocked his white sailor's cap further down over his white eyebrows and shuffled back to his kitchen.

What came out of Andreas's frying pan that day was, as Anghelos said, as good as a poem. A special barrel of wine had been tapped in his honour. He claimed that it was like the nectar of the gods. The only thing that cast a shadow over the meal was when Panaghiotis sat down at a nearby table. No one paid any attention to him, and the wine which Petros served him couldn't have come from the same barrel. After a while he got up and went away. They stayed on in the crystal sunlight, eating and drinking. Theo and Anghelos did most of the talking while the others listened.

They were about to rise from the table at last when Anghelos suddenly turned to Ersi. "Tell me, have you read any of my works?"

She shook her head. She was ashamed to admit that she had never glanced inside her mother's books of his poetry.

He told the severe lady, "Egeria, there must be a copy of *Reunion on Parnassos* in the car." She rose and went to fetch it.

When Egeria returned, he handled the book lovingly. He opened it, looking pleased at the way the type was arranged on its pages. "A book is like a house," he remarked. "It needs generous margins."

"What is this one about?" Ersi asked.

"It is a play in verse. I have tried to put down the conversation of the gods through the medium of men. Maybe, after you have read it you can tell me if I succeeded." He paused. Then he said, "Would you like me to inscribe it for you?"

"Oh, yes! Please!" It was the first time in her life that an author would be writing in his own book for her.

He wrote something across the flyleaf. "Read it later, when you are by yourself." He kept staring intently at her. "I think," he said at last, "that you must come up to Delphi. I can show it to you as few others can. You know about the Delphic Sibyl, don't you? She was the priestess of the oracle there. They would come from the remotest corners of the ancient world to consult her. She knew the past, the present, and the future." There was a twinkle in his amber eyes. "I maintain that the old woman still keeps her oracle running and that she never fails in her predictions. If we don't run into her personally, I can at least show you the place where her sanctuary was. Do you know what was cut over the entrance, deep into the stone?"

She shook her head.

"Two words: *Know Thyself.*" He rose to his feet. "Get Theo and Tiggie to bring you."

"When?"

"Better still, come by yourself. Even the best of uncles and aunts can cramp one's style."

Going alone would be more of an adventure! "When?" she repeated. "When can I come?"

He thought about it for a moment. "I will let you know." He reached for his hat, placed it on his head where it sat like a halo, gathered his cloak about him, motioned to his companion to take care of the bill, and floated off to the waiting car.

When they got home, Ersi raced upstairs with the book; Anghelos's script was broad and flowing, like Chinese calligraphy. He had written in English, "The poet lifts one corner of the curtain. Only a glimpse is given, no more. By it, the mind is fired to see what lies behind." Under that he had put his name, and the date.

Theo said that *Reunion on Parnassos* had been written nearly a decade ago. Since the Colonels came into power, Anghelos had not published anything.

"Why not?"

"Poets in repressive societies are forced to take words more seriously than writers who have the luxury of saying everything."

"You told me yourself that he had been a candidate for the Nobel Prize. The Colonels wouldn't dare to touch him, no matter what he wrote, and the whole world would listen. Shouldn't he publish something, at least as a protest?"

Anghelos had discussed it with Theo. Something might

be ready soon. "I hope so," Theo said. "He is one of the rare, true poets. In his poetry the Greek language carried you, as though on eagle's wings, into the fields of light. He has the divine fire."

Lefteris listened greedily when she told him about Anghelos Eliou.

"I saw him there with you," he said. "I knew who it must be."

"Why didn't you come up to our table? You could have met him."

He stared at her in astonishment. "How could I? What could I have said to someone like that, to a poet, a world-famous poet?"

Yet it was Lefteris whose quick eye caught the lines in the text of the book which the poet had underlined with a thick stroke of his pen. He read it aloud to her.

"'At a time when all friends are strangers,'" it said, "'the Gods will always send you a stranger for a friend.'"

15 *Kapetan Sarandis*

After that, Ersi kept turning her gaze towards the mountain. She wondered what Anghelos would be doing up there. She was waiting for the summons from Delphi. Or had he already forgotten his promise?

Theo was positive that now Anghelos was preparing a new work for publication.

"It's about time," Tiggie said. "His silent protest has lasted too long."

Meanwhile, Ersi and Lefteris had a new game. It consisted of watching the tourists who clustered around the tables on the quay. They had to guess where they came from. The rules were that you couldn't speak to them, and the tourists were not to suspect that they were being observed. Lefteris kept score.

On that particular day they had already spotted an Australian couple and a man who remained a mystery until he went to his car. It had Swedish plates. Lefteris said they were very rare in Greece.

They rode off along the quay feeling satisfied with their morning's work. They had almost reached the far end when a small caïque entered the harbour, a battered vessel with patched, faded sails. They stopped to watch it.

It wasn't long before the skipper came out onto the unwashed deck. He had a lean, bronzed face and grey stubble on his cheeks. A visored black captain's cap sat rakishly on his wiry grey hair. He was holding the end of a hawser. "Catch!" he called out.

Ersi was the one who caught it. He leaped down and fastened it to a bollard. She noticed how quick and clever his hands were. They were strong and very sunburned. Then he looked around him with the hard, sharp eyes of a bird of prey. "A sudden squall came up yesterday and swept my charts overboard. What port is this?"

Lefteris told him.

"That's a good thing. I was planning to make it my next landfall. And it means I'm getting closer to home."

"Is your home very far away?" Lefteris asked.

"Far enough. I wouldn't care to tell you how long it is since I last saw my wife and my boy. Telly looks like you, but he's older."

"I'll be fourteen," Lefteris said. "But I'm a little small for my age."

"Never mind. One of these days, before you even know it, you'll shoot up. Now, where can I have a glass of something?"

They pointed out Thymios's coffee shop. "That's the *kaffenion* of the Argonauts."

He stared at the tables. "Argonauts? Those old dodderers? There must be something better than that."

"Well, there's Bread and Salt's *taverna*," Ersi said.

"That's more like it. Come and sit with me, the two of you. I feel like talking. I've been alone with the sea and my own thoughts for too long."

Most of the tourists had already been served by then, so there were empty tables. They sat at the nearest one.

"What do they call you, son?"

"Lefteris."

"And you?"

"Ersi."

"It suits you. I would like to have had a daughter. As we

say on my island, 'A son is a son till he finds him a wife; a daughter's a daughter the rest of your life!' I am Kapetan Sarandis," he said. "From the Ionian Islands."

Petros appeared. Kapetan Sarandis said he wanted wine and something with which to line his belly. "And my friends will have . . ."

"I know what they will have," Petros told him, cutting him short. It was all too clear that he didn't approve of Ersi's sitting there with Lefteris and this raffish stranger. He came back with two *gazozas* and bread and wine. He set a dish down on the table. "Octopus in red wine sauce," he said. "You can eat it or leave it. It's all that's left in the kitchen."

"I'll take it. What could be better?" He offered forks to Ersi and Lefteris. They said that they had already eaten.

He ate with concentration, not saying a word. He had swallowed his first glass of wine in a single gulp, holding his little finger straight out. When he finished mopping up the last of the sauce with his bread, he shoved his plate away. He refilled his glass, emptied it, and wiped his moustaches with the back of his hand.

"That's what the sea does," he said. "It sharpens a man's appetite, just as it sharpens his heart and sharpens his brain." He lit a cigarette and leaned back.

"How long have you been at sea?" Lefteris asked.

"So long that my blood ebbs and rises with the tides. There must be salt in it by now, my boy, like the sea."

"You must have seen many wonderful things in your travels," Lefteris said hopefully.

"Ay, what have I not seen!" His eyes, which were like blue ice, fanned into fire as he spoke. "I have lived through the rage of Poseidon. I have heard the Sirens singing. I have even seen the Gorgon, the Great Mermaid. I saw her with my own eyes, and I spoke to her, just as I am speaking to you now."

He tapped another cigarette against the back of his

hand. "There are times," he went on, "when your ship sails by itself for whole days and nights at a stretch, struggling in faraway waters, with nothing around you but sky and sea, sea and sky. Night falls and day breaks, and there is still no sight of land. It is as though your ship has grown roots in the ocean.

"It was just such a time, the middle of August it was, around the Feast of Our Lady, and the moon was full. I was alone at the helm. All at once I heard a great commotion. It was as though some Leviathan of the sea was threshing the water with its tail. I tried to turn the tiller. It stayed nailed where it was.

"And then I saw her, the Gorgon, the Great Mermaid! She had heaved herself out of the waves and stood straight up in front of me. She was so immense that one of her hands rested on the helm and the other on the gunwale. As far as her waist she had the body of a woman. From the waist down she was like a fish, all scales. She looked like a ship's figurehead, except that a figurehead is smaller and is carved out of wood, while she was all flesh and blood. Her eyes shone like stars in the night. Her hair streamed from her temples like writhing tentacles. Around her neck she wore a garland of shells and seaweed.

"I knew at once who she was. Every seaman has heard of her. I held on to my courage, made the sign of the cross three times, and waited. I had stopped breathing.

"Then the Gorgon spoke. So long as I hold my breath, I will never forget that voice. It was like thunder, and at the same time, infinitely sad.

"'How fares my brother, the Great Alexander?' she said. 'Does he still live?'

"I had heard about the Great Mermaid and her ways, so I knew what answer to give. I cried out as loud as I could, 'He still lives and reigns, my lady!'

"And that was it. No sooner had I said the words than she let go of the ship and sank slowly, slowly, down into the sea. You must understand that she is the sister of Alexander the Great, and she wanders all over the ocean asking the sea captains and the skippers about him. Every seaman knows the answer to her question. If he doesn't know how to respond properly, well, it's tough luck for him."

"What happens then?" Ersi asked.

He took a long drag on his cigarette and blew the smoke out of his nostrils. "There was this young captain from Patras. You know what they are like in Patras. They think they know everything. When she puts the question to him, he told her, 'Alexander the Great? My dear Madam, where have you been all this time? He died two thousand years ago, in Babylon, of a fever.' The Great Mermaid just closed her hands around his ship and crushed it as though it was nothing more than a matchbox."

Kapetan Sarandis was looking at them in an odd way. "I know what you must be thinking," he said. " But I assure you that she was real. I had heard about her from sailors who had travelled all over the seven seas, as well as some seas that no one has ever heard of. Still, I never dreamed that I would see her with my living eyes. In this life, by the Gods, you never know what is a dream and what is actually so." He gulped down the last of the wine from the carafe. "Yes, that's so, by the Gods!" he said.

He pushed back his chair, got to his feet and threw some money onto the table. "Well, I'm off. I have to find the harbour-master and some new charts as well. Then I have to get my caïque ready."

"And then?"

"And then there's a little job I have to do, somewhere in the neighbourhood."

"Do you ever go as far as England?" Lefteris asked him.

"Who can tell? In this life, you never know, by the Gods!"

"Will we see you again?" Ersi asked.

"Maybe!" he called back as he went off along the quay. He could have been a pirate, she thought, if there had been a sabre or a cutlass in his hand instead of a string of amber worry beads. She turned to Lefteris. She suspected what he was thinking. "Would you go with him?"

"Where?"

"I don't know. Anywhere."

"Oh, yes." His eyes had a faraway look.

"To England, maybe?"

"Especially to England," Lefteris said.

Later, she saw that the caïque was gone from its mooring. She barely reached the harbour in time to see it, its sails spread, heading out into the open gulf. Before it vanished over the edge of the horizon she managed to make out its name and its home port painted on the stern: THE PENELOPE. ITHAKA.

Petros was sweeping the sidewalk in front of the *taverna* as she passed it on her way home. "I have something for you," he called out. He jerked his chin in the direction of the table where they had sat with Kapetan Sarandis. A parcel lay there, wrapped in newspaper. "He left it for you."

"Didn't he say anything?"

"Only that it was a gift from the sea."

"Nothing else? Try to remember."

Petros scratched his head. "Something crazy, about his leather bag being filled with the four winds, and he had to be on his way while they still held favourable. He's probably off on some tricky deal, like running contraband to Italy. Who can believe anything those old sea wolves say? They're a sly lot, full of lies and tricks, every last mother's whelp of them."

She took the parcel home. She cut the grimy string and tore the wrapping away. Inside the yellowed sheets of newspaper lay a curious, whorled shell. Its inner side was pearly, tinged with a deep pink.

Just then Theo walked in. "That's a chambered nautilus, a rare object for these parts. Mostly they're found in tropic seas. Where on earth did you find it?"

"A sea captain I met on the quay gave it to me."

He held it up to her ear. "Listen!" he said.

She could hear a low, restless murmur, like the pounding of the sea.

Theo was smiling to himself, intoning some words she could not understand.

"What was that?"

"That was ancient Greek, from Homer. 'Tell me, Muse, of the man of many wiles, who wandered far and wide . . .' It is the opening line of the *Odyssey*. Perhaps," he said, "what you were listening to just now was the same song that Odysseus heard when the Sirens sang to him."

16   *A Reunion in Delphi*

The message came early the next morning. Anghelos would be waiting for her at the Coffee House of the Nine Muses in Delphi from eleven until noon.

But how would she get there? Thanasis's taxi had already been booked by a party of tourists who were going in the other direction. The bus left too late. Theo said that a bus schedule was something a poet might tend to disregard.

"It's no problem," Ersi said. "I'll go on Pegasus."

"All that way?" Tiggie said. "And uphill?"

"I'll start early."

"Stop fussing, Tiggie," Theo told her. "At her age you'd have done the same thing and thought nothing of it."

Tiggie gave in, but only after Ersi had promised several times over to be careful on the curves and to stay on the edge of the road. Greek drivers were so wild! Before Ersi went off, Tiggie placed a parcel in the basket of the bicycle, containing some little cakes that Anghelos particularly liked. There was also a sheaf of flowers from the garden, wrapped in dampened newspaper to keep them fresh.

"The sun will be high. Don't forget your straw hat."

"It never stays on."

"It will this time. I sewed an elastic band inside."

They stood at the garden door and waved her away.

She wished that Lefteris was going along with her, but Anghelos's invitation had only been for her.

Drivers waved as they shot past her on the road. She stopped to rest in a vast olive grove, cooling off in the deep green shade. After that, when the going got steep, she walked Pegasus. She could look down and see the sea. The sun glinted on its surface like a sheet of rippled gold. The village looked like a collection of toy houses. Just outside Delphi she caught sight of something small and dark lying on the verge of the road.

She thought, "Oh, don't let it be some poor animal that got run over!" If it was, that would be a bad omen. If it wasn't, everything would go well that day in Delphi.

It turned out to be a strip of jagged rubber from a blown-out tyre. She coasted into Delphi without even having to pedal.

The Coffee House of the Nine Muses was at the very top of everything, overlooking the ancient ruins. The square was shaded by great plane trees. There was the sound of rushing water everywhere. Was she really at the centre of the world, at its very navel?

From the tables rose a babel of voices. She propped Pegasus against the trunk of a tree and looked for Anghelos. She could not see him anywhere.

What she did see was the lady of the bus, the Python Lady, sitting with a man whose face Ersi could not make out.

At the same moment, the Python Lady saw her. She rose and proceeded towards her with a stately, purposeful tread. "I was expecting you," she said in a low voice.

"Me?" Ersi exclaimed.

"Don't bother to ask why. I just knew you were coming. And now that I see you here, I know that you are exactly the person we need."

Ersi recalled the Python Lady's bewildering tendency to make extraordinary statements. She drew Ersi aside. "I know why you are here today," she said, "but first I want you to take a good look at those two men at the next table."

They looked like two ordinary Greeks who were drinking Turkish coffee and smoking cigarettes. In their dark suits, sombre ties, gabardine coats and felt hats, they might have been undertakers' assistants. Yet there was something about them that reminded her of someone she had encountered before.

Panaghiotis! Even to the pointed shoes!

"Do you know who they are?" the Python Lady was saying.

"I can guess."

"Let me just say that they are here because of someone whose name I do not have to mention, a friend of yours."

Anghelos? What did they want with him?

The person who had been sitting with the Python Lady now got up and joined them. It was the man who had met her at the airport in Athens, the one with the little silver wings in his lapel. "Miss Lewis!" he said. "I remember you very well. You must be wondering what am I doing here. I have my work to do. I welcome the new arrival. I speed the departing guest. Hermes Travel Agency."

The Python Lady asked him in a low voice, "What is he doing now?"

"He is still inside with his Egeria." His mouth twitched with exasperation. "It is impossible to get him to move. I told him there was no time to lose, that I had made the arrangements to get his manuscript out of the country, that it was the only way to get it published. He merely waved me off. He is still in there, at his usual table, writing. He says he cannot relinquish the manuscript before he has added some last words. Meanwhile . . . "

"Meanwhile," put in the Python Lady, "there are others who have come here who plan to take him away as well, along with his manuscript. We have to make sure he does not fall into their hands. Otherwise . . . "

"Otherwise what?" Ersi asked.

"Possibly house arrest, but more likely it will be some barren island in the middle of the Aegean Sea, with no paper to write on and no pen to write with."

"Would they dare? To him?"

"They would dare to do anything. They have the power."

They had done it to Solon. Now it was Anghelos's turn.

"But they can't just get rid of everyone who doesn't agree with them!" She almost heard her father's voice saying what she had so often heard him exclaim: "That's no way to run a government!"

The Hermes man said thoughtfully, "There is only one hope."

"I have already thought of that," the Python Lady said. She turned to Ersi. "That is where you come in, my dear girl. You have to help us stop them."

"Me?" Ersi stared at her. "But how?"

"We haven't thought of exactly how, but . . . "

Ersi was thinking of Solon. How could she let the same thing happen to Anghelos?

"Listen," she said. "If they come by car, I could get in front of it when the moment comes and block them before they can take him away."

"You want to jump in front of the car?"

"Why not? I could manage to fall off my bike."

The Python Lady considered. "All right," she agreed, quickly. "But don't be afraid. Nothing will happen to you. I promise. I know you will manage beautifully. But you must wait until I give you the signal."

"What signal?"

"I will rattle my bracelets."

Just then a murmur spread through the crowd. They

turned to look. Anghelos Eliou and his Egeria stepped through the door of the Coffee House of the Nine Muses.

The sound swelled. Every Greek there knew who he was. The murmur was different from the usual acclaim for a movie star or a popular singer or an athlete. No one ran up to ask for an autograph. No one called out. They turned their faces towards him. It was as though they were applauding him silently. He was their poet, a part at their language.

He did not see Ersi. Perhaps he had forgotten all about his invitation. The manuscript clutched in his hand, he seemed oblivious of all that was going on around him.

The men at the next table shoved back their chairs and got to their feet. Ersi could make out the bulges at their hips as they edged forward.

As Anghelos advanced through the maze of tables, the two men raced down to a large black car which stood parked just below the coffee house. One of them jumped inside, turned on the engine and revved it. The other waited beside the car. At the same time the Hermes man slipped down to the road where his own little car waited. He got into it and pulled up until he was level with the other.

After that everything happened quickly. One of the two men said something in an undertone to the poet. Anghelos jerked away. The Colonels' man leaned against him, pressing something into his side. Anghelos and Egeria were hustled into the car.

The Python Lady jangled her bracelets: Ersi's signal.

She vaulted onto Pegasus. The black car shifted into gear. The bike hurtled forward. She wobbled the front wheel and managed to crash to the ground a few feet in front of the car, just as it began to move. She dropped to the road as limply as a glove. Flowers and little cakes were strewn all over the asphalt. Her hat rolled away like a cartwheel and came to a stop in some bushes, yards away.

The Python Lady ran forward. "I told you you could make it! You're not hurt, are you?"

"No. I just feel as though all my batteries were turned off."

"Then stay where you are."

The Python Lady advanced towards the black car on her swollen feet. Her scarabs rattled menacingly. "Scoundrels!" she screamed. "Gangsters! Running down a child like that! You've killed her!"

The men leaped out of their car. They waved their arms. It wasn't their fault, they shouted. Someone ran to help Ersi. Someone else called out for an ambulance. Meanwhile, the Hermes man yanked Anghelos, his companion, and the manuscript, out of the car, shoved them into his, and whisked them off.

Ersi heard the shrilling of sirens. The local police had arrived. Explanations were demanded. Evidence was volunteered. Names were taken down. Finally, the two men took their local colleagues inside to reveal their official identities. By then it was too late. The poet, his Egeria, and the manuscript were well on the road that was to take them away from Delphi and outside the country, to safety.

The Python Lady was bending over her. "I didn't expect you to do it quite so recklessly. Are you sure you're all right?"

Ersi sprang up. "I feel wonderful!", and the Python Lady laughed.

She hadn't been afraid, she told herself, not for a moment. She had finally done something against the Junta. And she couldn't wait to tell Lefteris about it.

The Python Lady spoke to the local policemen. They dispersed the crowd. The two Junta agents disappeared in their black car. An open truck had just rolled up. It belonged to a pedlar who travelled to all the surrounding villages, hawking his wares from the back of it. A loud-speaker was attached to the top. He had not planned to go down the mountain that day, but the Python Lady decided that he was going to do so now. They found Ersi's hat, but the flowers and the cakes were beyond rescue. The driver hoisted Pegasus onto the back of his truck where it rested among the pink and red and blue and yellow and green plastic jugs and basins. Ersi was helped up in front beside him.

The Python Lady waved her bracelets in farewell and they were off.

As the truck rocked down the mountain, she felt as though she were in a circus wagon. The loudspeaker blared its music all the way.

She hadn't seen the museum of Delphi or the marble temples or the place where the words *Know Thyself* had been chiselled into the stone over the door of the Sibyl's sanctuary. Anghelos had also promised her a glimpse of the Delphic Sibyl herself. She was sorry most of all to have missed that. Well, the Python Lady would have to be the next best thing.

The driver dropped her and Pegasus off at the village square.

As she climbed back onto the bicycle she realised that, for once, the Python Lady had been wrong. *"They depart. We will remain,"* she had said in the bus on the way from Athens. The truth was that Solon and Anghelos had departed while the Colonels still remained.

So much for the Python Lady, with her air of being someone who knew the All.

There had been something else that Ersi had wanted to ask her. "You will find the person you are looking for," she had promised. What had the Python Lady meant by that? It couldn't have been Lefteris.

Tiggie and Theo listened intently while she told them what had happened.

"It's just what Ismene would have done if she'd been there," Tiggie remarked.

Ersi said, after a silence, "I remember how she once told my father, when they were talking about his work, that it was a wonderful thing to have a chance to act, to do something that matters. 'Most people,' she said, 'never have the chance.'"

She saw Tiggie and Theo exchange one of their looks.

"Well," Tiggie said, "now you know for yourself how it feels, don't you?"

Which was exactly what Lefteris said when she told him what had happened. From the rueful way in which he said it, she knew how much he wished that he was the one who had been given the chance to help rescue Anghelos Eliou from the Colonels' men.

17 *Philemon and Baucis*

Summer arrived suddenly, as though it had pounced.

You didn't hear the far reedy flute of Vassilis these days as he made his way over the hill with his flock. Instead, the sound of *bouzouki* music floated across the air. Someone had given him a transistor radio.

"So we won't be hearing it any more, that lovely wooden flute that Vassilis made himself?" Ersi said. "I'll miss it."

"We will all miss it," Tiggie said.

"True," Theo admitted. "But the radio's still music, isn't it? It still keeps Vassilis's loneliness away."

"But something seems to have gone from the village," Ersi said. "His flute is already part of the past."

"It doesn't make all that much difference," Theo told her. "Vassilis will still take his flock out in the morning and lead it home at night. Nothing ever really changes."

The days were very long now, but there was still not enough time to squeeze everything into them. The pomegranate trees were already covered with waxy coral-coloured blossoms that fell off if you brushed them accidentally. Ersi's hair had grown out, almost to its old length. "You look like a new girl," Tiggie said.

In the coffee houses, they were still talking about

Cyprus. Every day, practically, there was some item in the papers about new clashes between the Greek and the Turkish Cypriots.

And the swimming had begun. Most people went when the sun was high and hot. She could never wait until then. She liked to go early, by herself, when no one else was around. At first she would gasp with the shock of the cold water. Then she would rise to the surface, take a deep breath, and burst into the world. Her mouth, nostrils and eyes filled with brine and tingled with life. Little spotted fish darted at her to nibble at her legs, and when she came ashore the crabs scurried over the rocks and hid, watching.

Her father wrote to ask when she was coming home. It was already well into July. She would have to start thinking about going back to school.

Soon she would have to start saying goodbye to everything, but not yet. Not yet! She found herself looking at everything as though it might be for the last time. There were the little fishes, for instance, that slipped through the fishing nets on the quay and flopped about in the sun, glittering like sequins. She pushed them back into the water with her foot when she thought no one was looking.

The tourists had multiplied overnight, and there was no room for the regulars to sit at the Argonauts' coffee house. Some of the tourists looked like a strange warrior race that had come down from the North, with their motorbikes snorting and their fair hair streaming out from under helmets. Theo said they reminded him of the Crusaders who stopped to rest on these shores on their way to the Holy Land. "To the Greeks of the Middle Ages they must have seemed like another race, from another world."

"The Middle Ages!" Tiggie sniffed. "The young don't care about history. Today is enough for them."

"I'm not so sure. Isn't there some other time, Ersi, that you would like to have lived in?"

"Oh, yes!"

"You see, Tiggie? When?"

"The time before I came," she said. "My mother's time."

One day when she returned home with the newspaper there was a private but visible tension in the air. Tiggie was lighting a fresh cigarette, while another, still unstubbed, smouldered in the ashtray. Theo was pretending to be absorbed in a book.

"Your aunt and I," Theo announced, "are having a small divorce."

"Not so small," Tiggie put in. "It's serious this time."

"How serious?" Ersi asked.

"At least a twenty-five minute one."

Ersi tried not to smile.

Theo maintained silence behind a screen of pipe smoke. Tiggie said, "It's that compost heap of his. It's a positive obsession with him. He spends all his time breaking up bits of foliage and throwing them onto the pile. It's a wonder he doesn't put them in the blender first. And he's forever weeding, stooping in the sun when he shouldn't. Look at him now. He's all short of breath. I had to make him stop and sit down. He keeps forgetting that he's an old man."

He glared at her. "I'm not an old man."

She said gently, "Look in the mirror, Theo."

His mouth twisted into a rueful grin. "That's the whole trouble. I charge along throughout the day feeling like a young sprig of ... well, say thirty at the most. And suddenly I am confronted with some blasted mirror. And I say to myself, 'Theo, who is that aged – no, elderly – stranger? It can't possibly be you.' But it is. Ah, old age, the illness from which there is no possible recovery!"

Ersi regarded them as they sat across from her. It was as though she had never really looked at them before. She could see how twisted and gnarled with arthritis Tiggie's hands were, her rings loose on her fingers. Her neck was all folds and wrinkles. Theo's eyes suddenly looked washed-out and pale, his body thin and stooping under his loose jacket. His cheeks sagged, and he had been coughing a lot lately. She turned her face away. Why can't they stay just as they are, now? Don't let them get any older, she thought. Don't let them die, ever, please!

Theo was saying, "When you are young, you should live as though you were going to die tomorrow; when you are old, as though you were going to live forever. After all, death only happens to you once, and it lasts for such a long time. When the time comes, I think you must be ready to let go, to say goodbye ..." He looked around, almost anxiously, "... even to your garden. But we're not ready yet, are we, Tiggie old girl?"

"Personally," Tiggie said, "I can't possibly die before I'm eighty."

"Why not?" Ersi asked.

She smiled. "Because by then I'll be perfect."

"What worries me most," Theo said, "is who'll do the chores for you after I'm gone."

"Nonsense, Theo. I'm the invalid. I'll die first."

Theo turned to Ersi. "Your aunt is never going to die. Do you know what is going to happen when Charon, who collects the souls of the dead, comes to claim her?"

"That's enough, Theo." Tiggie made an impatient gesture in the air. "We have all heard it a thousand times."

"Ersi hasn't," Theo said. "She is going to say to him, 'Old Ferryman, what's your hurry? Let me just sit here quietly and smoke one more little cigarette before I go.' In the end he will simply give up."

"Just listen to him!"

"Anyway," he went on, "we are going to go together. How? Perhaps in an aeroplane, after a trip where we did everything we wanted to do and spent all our travellers' cheques. It will be a quick, clean crash, before we even

151

realise what has happened. Or maybe we will be like Philemon and Baucis."

"Like who?"

"Don't you know the story?"

"More mythology," murmured Tiggie, looking resigned.

"Once," Theo began, "Zeus and Hermes came down to earth in the guise of wayfarers, asking for food and a place to rest. They knocked everywhere. No one unbarred his door to let them in. Since all travellers who ask for shelter in a strange place are under the special protection of Zeus, this story of inhospitality made them more and more angry. They were ready to give up when they reached a small thatched cottage.

"At once a cheerful voice called for them to come inside, whoever they were. An elderly couple greeted them with smiles and made a place for them near the fire. The old man's name was Philemon. His wife was called Baucis. They had lived side by side for so long that they were like the two halves of the same scissors.

"They shared their evening meal with them. 'This is all we have,' they said, 'but you are more than welcome to it.' Philemon kept an eye on the wine, making sure that his guests' cups were always filled. No matter how much wine he poured out, the pitcher remained full.

"The old couple understood then that their guests were not ordinary wayfarers, but heavenly visitors. They fell on their knees before them.

"Zeus raised them to their feet. 'You have been hosts to the Immortal Gods. Now what favour would you like to ask of us?'

"Philemon said, 'We have passed our lives in love and concord. Let neither of us live on alone. We ask that one and the same hour will take us both from life; that I may not live on to see Baucis's grave, nor be laid in my own by her.'

"The Gods departed. One day, when Baucis and Philemon had grown very old and sat talking together about their life which had been so long, so hard, and yet so happy, Baucis saw that Philemon's body was putting forth leaves. And Philemon saw that his wife was changing in a similar manner. A layer of bark travelled slowly upwards to cover their old limbs. A crown of leaves already circled their heads. 'Farewell, dear heart!' each cried out to the other, and an instant later the bark had covered up their lips. They had become trees, a linden and an oak. But they were still united, both were growing from the same trunk."

"A very nice story," Tiggie conceded.

"What happened to the other villagers, the inhospitable ones?" Ersi asked.

"They were all drowned as a punishment."

"That was too much of a price to pay for not being able to cope with unexpected guests," Tiggie said. She looked sideways at Theo and laughed. The divorce was over.

18   *The Dogs of War*

They were aroused first thing the next morning by a shout
from Theo. He was already outside, in the garden.

"Tiggie! Ersi! Come and look!"

They ran out, still in their nightgowns.

Overnight, the amaryllis had burst into bloom. Now it
was crowned with two immense, perfect flowers, each of
creamy white ribbed with deep crimson.

They had breakfast in the garden in order to revel in the
sight of it. The wasps zoomed like kamikaze planes over
the butter and the honey.

Tiggie waved her arms about to discourage them. "They
are a positive plague!" she exclaimed.

Theo said that they were more like warnings. "Eat all the
honey you can, before it's too late!"

Sitting there between them in the dazzling morning sun,
with the scent of rosemary around them, spooning honey
onto her toast, Ersi thought, "This is what absolute happiness must be like." If the Gods had asked her to choose
one day of her life that would last forever, she would have
cried out, "This one! This one!" She would write down the
date so that she would never forget.

It was Saturday, the twentieth of July, in the year A.D.
1974.

Theo turned to her. "Of all the things in this house," he

asked, "what would you most like to take with you when you go home?"

Did he really mean that? She didn't even have to stop and reflect. She glanced towards Tiggie. Tiggie smiled at her, as though she and Theo had already talked about it.

"The little spoon rack!" Then she broke off. "Or would that be too much?"

"Is that all?"

Her mind roved over all the objects in the house. There were so many things she loved, but the spoon rack most of all. "I think so," she said.

She was not sure from the expression on Theo's face whether he was pleased or disappointed. He said, "In that case, we will have to see what we can do about it."

Absolute happiness became even more absolute, if such a thing were possible.

A little while later, Tiggie discovered that there were no eggs in the house. Would Ersi mind going off to the store? At the same time she could get a loaf of bread from the baker's. "But don't eat half the crust on the way home as Ismene used to do all the time!"

It was only when she reached the door of the Nettle's shop that she realised that there was something extraordinary in the air, a sense of turmoil all up and down the street. The Nettle didn't even notice her, which was unusual enough because he always had a special smile for her. He stood in the doorway among the crates of fruit and vegetables, his gaze fixed on his son who carried a suitcase and was squeezing into a car filled with young men from the village. Tears streamed down the Nettle's cheeks.

"Is he going back to his ship?" Ersi asked.

"What?" He blinked at her. "What's that you're saying? Haven't you heard? There's a general call-up."

She gaped at him. What did he mean?

"All the men of fighting age are being mobilised," he said. "They have to report to their units for military service. A Greek Cypriot, a Junta man, has overthrown the existing government in Cyprus. So the Turks have flown troops in. They say they have to protect the Turkish population there. We may be at war any minute."

It was no time to ask him for eggs. She went up the street, trying to take in what he had said. All around her, men with suitcases or flight bags or just parcels wrapped in brown paper carried under their arms, were leaving the village. The young ones were laughing. The older men wore set faces.

She saw Lefteris, standing by himself. He looked stricken. She ran up to him.

"What is going to happen now, Lefteris?"

"Who knows? If there is a war, how will I ever be able to rejoin my family?"

Most of the stores had rolled down their shutters. The bakery was locked. Ersi and Lefteris made their way to Dragonas's mini-supermarket on the square. It was still open, but it was impossible to get through the door.

"Look at them!" Lefteris said. "You'd think they'd be ashamed."

People were swooping into the store where they swarmed about, snatching up tins of sardines, cans of evaporated milk, packets of macaroni, sugar, toilet paper, anything they could pull off the shelves. They heard a scream. Lefteris squeezed in to see what had happened. A woman had fainted. She had been slapped in the face by another woman during their struggle over a jar of mayonnaise.

Ersi stood there, unable to believe what was happening. How had they remained unaware of it all, sitting in the garden and eating toast and honey? Cars filed out of the village. Face after face that she knew flashed by. She saw Stathis, the barber, zoom past on his motorbike with

Manolis, the electrician's assistant, perched behind him. Even Thanasis and his taxi had been mobilised.

There was a deafening roar in her ears. It could only be the enemy airforce coming over in a wave to bomb the village! She closed her eyes and waited to see her whole life race through her mind like a speeded-up television re-run. They said that was what flashed in front of you the moment before you died.

She did not see anything, only a vague glow of colour. Sunfish swam across her tightened eyelids. Nothing happened.

She let her eyes open. She saw a rush of black metal and black leather surge out through the square, trailing a cloud of dust and exhaust fumes. It was only the motorcycle tourists, getting out of the village, out of Greece, while the going was good.

"I have to go back now," she told Lefteris.

He nodded blankly. She ran off to tell Tiggie and Theo the news. The world had broken into thousands of pieces.

From the look on their faces she saw that they already knew.

Theo said, "We are concerned about you."

"About me?"

"It looks serious. I tried to get in touch with your father from the telephone office. The lines are all tied up. There is no way to get through to anywhere, least of all overseas. We will have to wait and see what we can do about you."

She was about to reply that they didn't have to do anything about her, when he burst out, "I know! There happens to be someone in the village from Athens just now. He's here on other business, but he might just be able to do something for us."

"How can you find anybody in all this confusion?" Ersi asked.

But Theo was already off.

He wasn't gone long. When he came back he

announced, "There's a vessel leaving Greece very shortly. I have arranged everything. The Captain will be taking Ersi with him."

"With him? Where?"

"To Italy. You can get a flight to New York from there. The Athens airport is closed. This is no place for you to be if a war breaks out. You had better get packed right away."

"I have to run and say goodbye to someone first."

"There isn't time for that now."

"But . . ."

He shook his head. There was nothing to do but race upstairs and collect her things. She remembered to put Kapetan Sarandis's shell in her bag, tucked under the scarf Tiggie had given her for Easter, along with Anghelos's book.

"Do you have everything?" Tiggie asked when she came downstairs.

"I think so."

"What about your bathing suit?"

"Oh, I forgot. It must be out on the line."

"Exactly like Ismene." Tiggie handed it to her. "It's dry enough to go in your bag."

And there was Pegasus, propped against the wall. She would have to leave it behind, as a kind of hostage. When would she come back to claim it?

"Do you have your plane ticket?" Theo asked.

"Yes."

"And your passport?"

She had that, too.

"What about money?"

She nodded. She still had most of the travellers' cheques her father had given her as a going-away present.

"Then we'll have to get moving," Theo said. "We can't keep the others waiting."

She turned to say goodbye to Tiggie.

"I'm coming with you," Tiggie said.

"The boat is at the end of the quay," Theo told her. "It's
a long walk."

"Don't be silly. Of course I'm coming."

As they were leaving the garden, Theo pressed something into Ersi's hand. "It's rosemary."

"I know," she said. "For remembrance. Did you think
I'd need it?"

The quay was deserted. Halfway along they had to stop
while Tiggie caught her breath. As they waited, she saw
Lefteris come running towards them. There was a fresh
carnation in the pocket of his shirt. The books she had lent
him were under his arm. He had come to return them. But
how had he learned that she was going away?

Then she caught sight of the old leather suitcase he was
lugging. Behind him came the Hermes man.

"Lefteris is leaving with you," Theo told her quietly.
"Old Marigoula can't take care of him any more. He
should have left a long time ago. My friends from the
Hermes Agency arranged everything, including his ticket,
which is paid for. I must say I didn't expect him to take
care of it quite so soon."

"We do our best," the Hermes man said with a quick
smile. "I was planning to take the boy back to Athens with
me and put him on a plane to London there. But since
there are no planes, it was fortunate that I ran into an old
acquaintance, someone who had worked on several pro-
jects with me in the past. He just happened to be around in
these waters."

Lefteris was too breathless to say anything, but his eyes
shone. He thrust the books at Theo.

"Keep them, my boy," Theo said. "They're yours if you
want them."

The Hermes man handed Lefteris a long envelope. "This
has everything you need. As soon as you reach Italy, call
your father, and reverse the charge. The number is written

down. Don't thank me. Just have a safe trip. And you too, Miss Lewis." He gave her a slight bow of his head and a smile of special complicity. "Now I must be off. I have a lot to do these days. Here comes your boat." He vanished. No one saw him go, but there was the sound of a car starting up and driving off.

How had Theo known about Lefteris and the books? There was no time to ask. The boat was coming towards them. It was a dark, sea-beaten caïque with a hawk-faced figure standing in the prow. By the time they reached the end of the quay he had pulled the boat alongside.

"By the Gods," Kapetan Sarandis called out, "we meet again! Are you two my passengers? Jump aboard, there's no time to lose." He reached for their things and set them down on the deck. Lefteris leaped on board after them.

Theo turned to Ersi. "This is it," he said. "Get in touch with your father as soon as your flight is confirmed in Rome. I'll try to get through to him myself as soon as the lines are clear."

They kissed her. "Goodbye for now, my child," Tiggie whispered. Her voice was very controlled. It was hard to let go. In the end, Kapetan Sarandis reached out, picked Ersi up by the waist as though she were a flowerpot and placed her on the deck of his caïque. The next moment they were moving off.

"Goodbye, Miss Rosy Fingers!" Theo called from the shore. "Come back soon. We will be waiting for you."

Tiggie and Theo stood very close together, waving. They looked smaller every moment. As she waved back she could see the village, the white-washed houses, the barren rock, the sky. The sea was widening between them. She thought, I want to stay here always. She felt as though she had been there forever. But it was no longer *here*. It was already *there*. She could smell Theo's rosemary on her hands. She thought of the sleeping girl she had seen on the old tomb in the village cemetery, so real and lifelike that you expected her to wake up and look at you. Now she was leaving that girl behind.

She glanced towards Lefteris. He took the red flower from his pocket and tossed it into the sea. His lips moved silently as he watched it bobbing on the surface of the water, away from them.

It was only when the village was a faint smudge, and even the sleeping giant was no longer visible, that she remembered the little spoon rack. They had forgotten all about it.

19 *Crossing the Gulf*

Kapetan Sarandis said they would have to put in at Patras long enough to clear the caïque's papers for Italy and to get Ersi's and Lefteris's passports stamped. "It's too bad we can't just slip through at night, without stopping."

A lot of foreign vessels were lined up at Patras, trying to get out of the country. He fumed and cursed, but it wasn't until Monday morning that he was finally able to run down an official he knew. He slipped him a few thousand-drachma bills along with their passports. Then they were free to set out across the gulf and out into the open Ionian Sea on their way to Italy.

Soon there was no sign of land anywhere. He fixed them something to eat in his tiny galley and then left them to themselves. "I have to stick to my tiller," he told them. "Just keep a sharp look-out. You might be lucky and catch a glimpse of the Great Mermaid."

All day the caïque chugged along under the blazing sun. At night they stretched out on deck, under the stars. They fell asleep to the rhythmic slapping of the waves against the sides of the *Penelope*.

The next day they hung over the rail for hours on end. There was no sign of the sister of Alexander the Great, but they passed the time watching the schools of dolphins that kept appearing alongside the vessel. The dolphins accompanied them for miles at a time, bounding and leaping over each other as though they were showing off for their special benefit.

Lefteris said that he didn't understand why the dolphins travelled in *schools*. They seemed to be having too much fun. "If I have another life, I am going to be a dolphin."

"You'll have to learn to swim first," Ersi reminded him. "All you do when you are in the water is dabble around, trying to keep your chin above the surface."

"If I am a dolphin I won't have to learn. I'll just know."

Kapetan Sarandis's voice interrupted them. "Come in here," he called from the galley. "Right away!"

The news from Athens was on the radio. The announcer's voice seemed to be coming from a scratchy old record with a crack in it. She could make out only an occasional word, but Sarandis and Lefteris listened intently. As soon as the broadcast was over, Sarandis snapped off the dial. He and Lefteris looked at each other in an odd way. Lefteris expelled his breath in a low, slow whistle.

"What was all that about, Lefteris?" she demanded.

"There isn't going to be a war with Cyprus now," Lefteris said. "And the Junta ..." He broke off and swallowed hard.

Ersi clutched at his arm. "What about the Junta?"

"It's finished now," Kapetan Sarandis said.

"Finished? What happened? What's the matter with your voices, the two of you?"

"It's all a little bit complicated," Kapetan Sarandis said. "Let me try to explain it to you as I understood it. With the whole country in arms, the foreign powers standing by ready to intervene, and our own military men not sure as to how to go on with the war, the Colonels panicked. So the old guard of the army, the ones who had always been against them, seized the opportunity. They acted. They called the exiled political leaders back to Greece. The radio says that everybody is supposed to stay calm until a new, constitutional government can be formed."

"Stay calm!" she cried. "They should be setting off fireworks!"

So it had happened at last. The country had broken out of its plaster cast. Solon was safe. She wanted to shout, to jump up and down, to grab their hands and dance all over the deck the way they had at Barba Kostas's on the day of the Resurrection!

But when she reached out her hand for Lefteris's, he just walked past it and went to the stern of the caïque. He stood there, looking bleak and alone. He blinked as he stared in the direction of Greece.

"Let him be for a moment," Kapetan Sarandis told her. "He has a lot to think about." He poured himself a glass of wine from the demijohn he kept in the galley. He swallowed it in a single gulp. "For that matter, so do we all, by the Gods!"

In her mind she could hear the voice of the Python Lady. She had been right, after all. The Colonels had departed. Her thoughts flew to those who had remained, to all those who would be returning from their long exile, like Solon. Now he could emerge from his silence. He could go back to his wife. He would be able to speak out openly again, and read Aristotle without being afraid of getting arrested for it.

She turned to Kapetan Sarandis. "And you, aren't you glad?"

He poured himself another glass of wine. "It means that my job is over now," he said. "No more running people out of Greece, like contraband goods. The last time I was in these waters I also had a couple of passengers. From the way Mr Hermes spoke to the man, I gathered that he was in the way of being an important personage. But during the whole trip he didn't speak a single word, not even to the lady who was travelling with him. I never found out who he was. In this business," he added with a canny wink, "it's better not to ask questions."

"When was that?"

"I can tell you exactly. It was the day after I ran into the two of you in the village. I picked them up in some deserted cove just below Delphi. They were on their way to Paris, in France. That was an exciting run!" His hawk's eyes gleamed. "They didn't have any papers on them at all, not even false ones."

"But that must have been Anghelos Eliou!" she cried.

"And who's he when he's at home?"

"Don't you know? He is Greece's greatest poet."

"I'm only a sailor, and not much of a man for reading." Kapetan Sarandis scratched his head. "All the same, I wish I'd known that. I could have told him a thing or two to put in his poems." He threw back his head, tossed the wine down his throat and wiped his mouth with the back of his hand. He seemed almost to regret that there wasn't going to be a war after all, and no more passengers without passports to smuggle out of the country.

Later, Lefteris crept around to where she sat on the deck by herself against a pile of ropes. She was wondering if the thin strip of land ahead of them could be Italy. He dug into her arm with his forefinger.

"I'm sorry," he said.

"Sorry about what?"

"You know. When you wanted to jump up and dance, and I wouldn't."

"Why wouldn't you?"

"I couldn't, just then. I didn't feel like it. I don't know what I felt like doing." He said hesitantly, "Maybe now?"

But the moment was gone. It was like being asked to celebrate your birthday after it was over.

That was Tuesday. The next morning Kapetan Sarandis shook them awake just as the sun was coming up. "Look over there, ahead of you, Italy!"

They rubbed their eyes and watched the land come slowly closer. In an hour they had reached the port. Kapetan Sarandis leaped ashore and lashed his caïque to the quay. "Wait here until I come back," he shouted, and plunged into the crowd. After a while he came back with a dapper little man who carried an attaché case. "This is Signor Mercurio," he said, "our man in Brindisi."

Signor Mercurio flashed them a dazzling smile.

"You're in his hands now," Kapetan Sarandis told them. "And now it's time for me to head home to Ithaka."

"I'm sure you must be looking forward to that," Ersi said.

"I guess so." His voice was hoarse. "It will be good to see my Penelope again, and the boy. I wonder about my old dog, Argos. Will he remember me after all this time?"

She and Lefteris shook hands with him and said goodbye, but as Ersi could see, Kapetan Sarandis was already thinking of Ithaka, and he was itching to set out on the last stretch of his journey home.

Signor Mercurio, who spoke English, said that there wouldn't be any of the usual problems, since all their papers were in order. He took care of everything with winged efficiency. He swept them through the passport controls and found a telephone booth from which Lefteris could call his father. Ersi watched Lefteris through the glass door. There was a tense expectancy on his face as he waited. Just then some people crowded outside the booth, awaiting their turn to use it, so she did not see him when he spoke to his father. It was just as well, she decided. It wasn't fair for anyone to be watching him at that moment.

"Imagine!" he said when he came out. "He knew my voice right away!"

Then Signor Mercurio drove them in his little Fiat to Rome. He took them straight to the airport.

There was a problem there about her ticket, since it was the high season and everything was booked. In the end,

Signor Mercurio wangled a seat for her on the first direct flight to New York. "You will get a refund there for the difference between Athens and Rome. Do not forget to insist."

She called her father from the airport. It was a poor connection. The only thing she managed to get through to him was the number and the time of her flight.

She offered to pay Signor Mercurio for his trouble. He held up his hands. "That will not be necessary, *Signorina*. Mr Hermes has taken care of everything. Here are your boarding cards." He flashed his dazzling smile again. "*Ciao*," he called out. "And *buon' viaggio!*", and left them there.

Lefteris's flight was scheduled to leave very shortly, half an hour ahead of hers. She went with him to the gate.

He turned to her, looking more earnest and solemn than ever. "I have to tell you something," he said.

"What, Lefteris? Hurry up. You'll be the last person on the plane!"

"It's this," he said slowly. "After all these years of waiting I'm not sure that I want to go." She gaped at him. "I'm afraid."

"Afraid? Of what? Of what you'll find there?"

"No," he said. "Maybe I'm afraid of what I won't find." Then he went through the gate.

"Goodbye, Lefteris!" she called after him. "Write to me!" But he didn't even turn to wave. He looked very small now as he raced down the ramp to catch his plane, even smaller than he had in the village.

20 *Evening Star*

She didn't even watch the movie on the plane. She slept all the way to New York.

The minute she emerged from the customs area at Kennedy Airport she heard her father's voice. "Carla!" She had grown so unused to the name that it almost sounded like someone else's.

He elbowed his way through the crowd and stood beside her, gripping her arms. "God!" he said, staring into her face. "It's so good to see you, Carla. I thought you were never coming back to me again."

She had never been so glad to see anyone in her life. Suddenly she realised how much she had missed him.

"I was worried about you," he was saying.

"About me? Why?"

"All those reports in the newspapers, and on TV. That business about Cyprus. I was ready to come over myself and collect you."

"There was no need. I just got on this caïque that took me to Italy, and I came home from there."

"You just got on a caïque! Surely there must be more to it than that. I have to hear the whole story, and about Tiggie and Theo and everything else that happened to you while you were away."

"I meant to bring you honey from Parnassos," she said,

"but in all the excitement, I forgot. And I have to tell you that now I understand what you meant when you used to talk about Alabama."

"Alabama? You mean you had to go all the way to Greece for that?" He was staring into her face. He said in a strange, choked voice, "Carla, you look . . . "

She smiled up at him. "How do I look?"

He considered. "Different," he said at last. "No, not really, come to think of it. You look like yourself, only . . . "

"Only older? Well, I am."

"It's not only that. It's something else." Then, slowly, he said, "You remind me of a girl I knew once when she came from Greece to go to college in America."

"Well," she said, "isn't that natural?"

As she said it, there was the Python Lady again, flashing through her mind. *"You will find the person you are looking for."* She understood now what the Python Lady, with her small sphinx of a cat, her scarabs, and her rattling bracelets, had meant.

It was as though she had found Ismene at last.

Her father bent and kissed her. He picked up her bags. "Let's find a taxi."

He didn't say anything all the way into the city. He only held her hand so tightly that it hurt. It wasn't until they had crossed the bridge and were in Manhattan that his grip relaxed. He reached out and cupped her chin in his hand. "You're home. I still can't believe it. And 'the Greek Experience', as your English teacher put it. How was it?"

"Perfect."

"Perfect?"

She glanced through the window of the cab, wondering what time it was here in New York. The evening star had already come out. Her watch was still set at the Aunts' time, in the village. It was seven hours earlier here. The

Greek Experience had happened in a different world, under a different sky.

"Perfect enough," she said.

21   *An Open Door*

Honor had come in for the day from Easthampton to see her. They met at their favourite hamburger place near Bloomingdale's.

After they had ordered, Honor leaned forward in the booth. "I can't wait, Carla. You have to tell me everything!"

"Well, it's a very small village," she began. "Most of the people there have lived in it all their lives. It's pretty, in a harsh kind of way, and people are friendly. Of course, we had the Colonels . . ."

"The colonels? Who are they?"

"They were the military dictators who had taken over the government," she said. Then she just sat there and looked at her. How could she explain what 'The Colonels' really meant?

After a moment Honor said. "At least you're home in time to come out to Easthampton before school starts. There's this boy I met. He plays great tennis, and we went to this party . . . Carla, you're not listening. You're a million miles away."

"Only in the village," Carla said, and blushed.

It was true. She had been thinking about the time she had encountered Kyria Dimitra with her daughter near the church of Aghios Nikolas. The sun was just setting. Kyria

Dimitra turned to her with a sigh. "Just look at that! Where else, my child, could you see such a sky, such colours in the sea, such a mountain!"

Her daughter cut her short. "Really, Mother! God has made a great many other places in the world, all of them just as beautiful."

"Oh, you are right, I'm sure. I have never travelled as you have, but I know that the wonders of the Almighty must be everywhere." Then she turned back to Ersi. "But tell me, my child, where else can you see such a sky, such a view as this?"

Where else, indeed!

Honor was waiting expectantly. "Would I like it, Carla?"

"I don't know, really, Honor," she said. "It's just a Greek village, like any other."

She went back to school in the autumn. Her special project, *The Greek Experience*, got high marks from Mrs Schoenberger, who even called her father to tell him how good it was.

By then the photographs of Ismene had reappeared in the apartment. She asked her father one day, "Do you think you might marry again?" He said, smiling, "I don't think so, Carla." She no longer avoided the Greek underground. Now she felt as though she were actually a part of it. And when a new girl at school remarked, in a friendly way, "You seem different from the rest of the girls in our class," Carla replied, "Maybe that's because my mother was Greek."

"Was?"

"Yes. She's dead."

The girl widened her eyes. "Oh. I'm so sorry . . . " she began.

"It's all right," Carla said. "I don't mind any more. Talking about her, I mean."

Greece for her now was a vanished world under a dazzling

sky. She kept planning to go back, but every summer something happened to prevent it. She wrote to Tiggie and Theo, however, at least once a month.

Theo always replied promptly, banging away on his old portable machine, with lots of mistakes. He passed on all the news of the village. Tiggie didn't write. She simply scrawled in Greek, in her large open handwriting, across the bottom of each letter, "I miss you, I kiss you." She had a postcard from Lefteris signed "The Cat", saying that he would write her a long letter soon, but she never heard from him again.

She was in her junior year in college when Theo wrote, "Old Barba Kostas ceased dancing the other day. Marigoula is gone. So is Demos. The church bells have been tolling a lot lately. Every time we hear them, your aunt and I feel closer to the day when they will toll for us. As it approaches, I mind about death less. I have decided that it is only an old door set in a garden wall.

"Meanwhile, in my mind, I travel among the constellations. I keep rereading Plato . . . The weather is changing. I am getting the Zodiac ready. When are you coming? It has been too long."

Under that, Tiggie had scrawled, as always, "I miss you. I kiss you."

There was no letter from them after that. She waited. She wrote twice.

One day a cablegram came from Greece. LOST IN THE ZODIAC, it read. LETTER FOLLOWS. The name of the sender was unknown to her.

The letter arrived, addressed to Miss Carla Ersi Lewis. It was written in formal Greek, and it bore the letterhead of a law firm in Athens.

"It is the sad duty of the undersigned to inform you that your aunt and uncle are now presumed to be dead . . ." They had gone out fishing one morning. A sudden squall had blown up. The little craft had been lost with them in it.

He went on to say that a certain household article, specifically a carved wooden rack for spoons, had been left to her in their will, along with the house which contained it and all its other contents. Some legal documents were enclosed. Would it be too much trouble for her to take them to the Greek Consulate in New York, sign them there in the presence of the Consul, and return them? Furthermore, would she please advise as to when she would be returning to Greece to claim her inheritance. He begs to remain, with respect, etc., etc.

She supposed she ought to burst into tears. Instead, she smiled. They had died as they had wanted to. She was distressed for herself, at the thought that she would never see them again. But she was glad for Tiggie and Theo, lost in the Zodiac together.

She wasn't able to get back until the autumn. She went alone. She did not want to return to the village for the first time with anyone else, not even her father.

She arrived there on a day when the first rains had washed away all the dust and the tourists and the summer visitors. Instead of the naked glare of July, when she had left it, there was a golden autumn haze in the air. Theo had always said it was his favourite time in the village.

A buzz of recognition rippled through the square when she stepped down from the bus. "Tiggie's American grandchild!" An old woman whom she did not remember reached out and pressed her hand. "Life for you," she said.

She made her way towards the house, along the back alleys so as to avoid the main street with the people and the shops. The Aunts greeted her from their window. "Time flies!" Kyria Stavroula cried. "We have been waiting and waiting for you. Sisters, look at her! She is already a young lady."

Barba Kostas's house was locked and shuttered. She

reached over the low wall to pick a carnation from the nearest flowerpot. It had the same sharp fragrance she remembered from that first morning.

There was no trace of the Colonels. New slogans were everywhere, new political initials daubed on the walls. She saw a sign proclaiming that the quay was now The Avenue of Democracy. She thought of Lefteris. What constituted one's country, she wondered? Its government? The place itself? Or was it, in the final reckoning, a state of mind?

She turned into the narrow cobbled street where the house stood. Someone came hobbling out to greet her. It was Kyria Dimitra. She enfolded her in her vast embrace. Her body had the same sweet and faintly acrid smell of earth and ripened fruit. "Life for you!" she said. "May you live to remember them! I will bring you some fresh bread in the morning."

She reached the faded pistachio-coloured door at last. The lawyer in Athens had given her an envelope with keys in it, after she had signed innumerable papers.

She set her bag down on the cobblestones. She found the big iron key and inserted it under the wrought-iron latch. She turned the great looped handle. It took both hands. The garden door swung open with a loud creaking of hinges, as it always had.

An explosion of green greeted her eyes.

Everything was overgrown. Dark red globes of fruit weighed down the branches of the pomegranate trees. She could smell the rosemary and the rose geranium. Was the garden, perhaps, smaller than she remembered it? Even though she knew it as well as her own hand, it seemed strange and unfamiliar.

She stood there, taking it all in with a gaze of slow recognition. A sharp pain cut through her chest. No, she could not bear it, this coming back without their being there.

After a moment she was aware of something that she

had never seen before. It was just beyond the rosemary hedge, near Theo's compost heap. She moved closer to look. There were two vines, one flowering with a pale blue flame, the other with a white one, so close together that they seemed to be growing out of the same stem, clasping each other.

Fighting back her tears, she knelt on the ground. With her bare hands she began carefully, lovingly, to clear the earth around the roots pulling up all the weeds and nettles that had sprouted there.

Then she got to her feet, took her bag, and walked slowly towards the house, the key in her hand.

Evening was falling. Soon it would be time for a small libation. Could she remember how the words went? Oh, yes. Yes! She repeated them under her breath. " 'Belovéd Pan, and all ye other gods that haunt this place . . . ' "

And in the morning, first thing, she would oil the hinges of the garden door.